THE ANGEL TEST

DARK WORLD: THE ANGEL TRIALS 7

MICHELLE MADOW

DREAMSCAPE PUBLI

D1409996

RAVEN

THREE MONTHS.

That was how long I'd been on Avalon, training for the Angel Trials.

Three months ago, I'd barely been able to run a mile without my lungs burning, my stomach cramping, and collapsing into a sweaty, red-faced heap on the ground.

Now I was completing the final lap around the track to finish running a marathon. Yes—an entire marathon. Twenty-six point two miles of running. And as I was coming around the final bend, I felt *great*.

I'd say there was something in the water here, except it would be no joke. Because the Holy Water we drank and the mana we ate definitely contributed to my body being able to complete feats it never would have been able to do three months ago.

But that was just a small reason why I was able to run this marathon today.

The main reason was that for the past three months, I'd been training my butt off. I'd been running five mornings a week, doing interval training four times a week, weapons training six days a week, and high intensity interval training on top of all of that.

For the first month and a half, I'd been exhausted. No, exhaustion was an understatement. I'd felt like I'd been run over by a truck. The only thing that had kept me going was the knowledge that my mom, Sage, everyone on Avalon, and everyone in the *world* was counting on me.

But after that halfway point, my body started to adjust. The workouts stopped being torture.

They started giving me energy.

I started feeling *strong*.

The cheering crowd watching me run the final part of the marathon fueled my strength. As I crossed the finish line, I raised my hands in the air, smiling in victory.

Noah ran toward me, picked me up, and twirled me around in a circle. "You did it." He lowered me down and kissed me—chaste enough that it was appropriate in front of the crowd, but passionate enough that I felt the slight brush of his tongue against mine. He tasted like the fresh forest, and I wanted more of him. I wanted *all* of him.

I also couldn't help being slightly self-conscious. Hopefully I didn't smell *too* bad after completing an entire marathon.

"You always smell delicious to me." He chuckled, gazing at me with those intense brown eyes that had stolen my heart the first time he'd kissed me in that grungy New Orleans bar. "Even when you sweat. *Especially* when you sweat." He raised an eyebrow, and my heart pounded faster than it had already been beating after running a marathon.

I hadn't spoken my thought aloud, but he must have picked up on it through the imprint bond. That happened sometimes when we were touching.

The connection between us would only intensify once we mated.

I couldn't wait.

My trainer, Darra, also stood nearby. She walked up to me, a giant grin on her face. Her teeth were bright white against her dark skin. "Congratulations, Raven!" she said, to both me and to the crowd watching us. "You've completed the first part of the Angel Trials. Tomorrow, you'll take a well-deserved day to rest. And the day after that… it's time to face the obstacle course and drink from the Holy Grail."

RAVEN

I WAS beyond restless the next day. How was I supposed to relax when I'd likely be drinking from the Holy Grail tomorrow?

I had no idea what to do with myself. Jessica and the other students were training on the supernatural training grounds. Noah trained students in the morning, and took his education lessons during the day. He was now able to read and write, and I was beyond proud of him. I knew he'd learn quickly.

Everyone else I knew decently well—Darra, Annika, Jacen, and the mages—were my superiors. They had their own jobs they were doing right now. As did Thomas and Bella. Thomas had gotten technology up and running on Avalon, so it no longer felt like living in the Middle Ages. But only the leaders of the island were allowed to communicate with the outside world. They were too worried about causing a mass panic if the supernaturals on Earth knew Annika had yet to turn any humans into Nephilim.

It would no longer be an issue after tomorrow, when I'd become the first human to drink from the Grail and survive. Hopefully. Everyone was putting on a positive face, but it was impossible to ignore the nervous energy buzzing through the island. Because even though my chance of survival seemed likely—since Rosella, the psychic vampire seer believed I was the one who could do this—psychics weren't *always* correct. The future was fluid and constantly changing.

There was still a chance I might die.

And so, I spent the majority of the day going on a ride with my unicorn, Annar. Galloping along the ground of Avalon—and across the water, too—I could let go of my worries about the future and focus on the present. It was just the two of us, enjoying the beauty of a utopian paradise.

Even after three months, being on the magical island of Avalon still blew my mind. I could get used to life here.

Which meant I definitely couldn't allow myself to die tomorrow.

Eventually the sun started to set, and Annar and I ran

back to the academy manor house. The other students were returning from the training grounds on their unicorns and wyverns at the same time as us.

I'd hoped to have a semi private dinner with Noah in the dining hall, at a table on the side, like we normally did. But we had no such luck.

Now that I'd completed the marathon and was attempting the next Trial tomorrow—the obstacle course—everyone at the academy suddenly wanted to be my best friend. They crowded our table, so busy talking about how the previous humans of Avalon had performed on the course that I couldn't get a word in myself.

Luckily, the imprint bond allowed Noah and I to communicate telepathically.

I thought the annoying perky blonde vampire hated you? he asked through the bond.

One glance at where he was looking confirmed he was referring to Samantha. She'd squirmed her way into one of the seats closest to me. Her two closest friends, Adriana and Ellen, surrounded her, as always.

I'd disliked them since they'd snubbed me my first day at Avalon. Especially Samantha. Jessica had used her gift and forced Samantha to say what she really thought about me, and those thoughts weren't pretty.

She does hate me, I answered. *But she wants to be the*

most popular girl at the academy. If I pass the Angel Trials, that'll probably make me the most popular. I shrugged, since popularity had never mattered to me. *I guess she thinks it'll earn her brownie points to be associated with me.*

Luckily I knew her true colors, and knew better than to trust her.

Not "if" you pass the Trials, Noah said into my mind. *When.*

Right. I corrected myself, since to have the best chance at passing, I needed to believe I could do it with every fiber of my being. *When I pass the Trials.*

He smiled, and I smiled back.

I loved how despite being surrounded by others, we could always escape into our own little world.

"All right, everyone," Darra said, bursting into the dining hall. "Raven has had enough excitement for the day. If she's going to perform her best tomorrow, she needs to get a full night's sleep." She looked pointedly at me, her message that I needed to retire to my quarters clear.

"Darra's right." I slid my seat back, more than happy to get away from the overly eager students around me. Noah's hand was in mine, and he stood up with me. "I need to head to bed."

"I'll make sure you get there safely," Noah said, accompanying me out of the dining hall.

Darra zipped in front of him, blocking his path. "No, you will not." She crossed her arms, as stern as ever. "Trainers aren't allowed in student quarters. You know the rules."

I shifted uncomfortably, aware that the room had gone silent. "Given the circumstances, I was hoping an exception could be made for tonight..." I said, trailing off when Darra's expression didn't change.

"No exceptions," she said, glaring at Noah. "And no distractions. The two of you will have plenty of time together *after* Raven completes the Trials. Unless you don't believe she's going to pass...?"

"No." Noah's expression hardened. "Of course she's going to pass."

"I thought so," Darra said, her gaze as strong as his. "But there's no need to worry about her getting to her quarters. I'll see her there myself."

As one of the head trainers of the academy, Darra was above the rules.

Noah gave me a long, intense kiss—which was sort of inappropriate given that we had an audience, but neither of us cared—and the two of us said good night.

3

RAVEN

I COULDN'T SLEEP.

All I could do was toss and turn, worrying about what would happen tomorrow.

What if I died without mating with Noah? Everyone seemed convinced I stood a chance at surviving, and I believed I had a chance, too. But nothing was a hundred percent.

I couldn't help thinking that waiting to mate with Noah was a mistake.

Yes, I hated the thought of my mom not being there to support me and give me away on the day I pledged myself to my soul mate. But I also hated the thought of dying without mating with Noah.

I'd been so focused on training these past few

months that I hadn't let it hit me until now. And now that it was, sleep was impossible.

It wasn't doing me any good to keep tossing and turning. And so, I got up, opened my wardrobe, and removed my cloaking ring from a small drawer inside. I hadn't needed to use the ring since getting to Avalon, since no one hid what we were around here.

But I didn't stand a chance of sneaking out of the manor house if the supernaturals could smell my distinctly human scent traipsing through the halls.

Since it was past midnight, everyone was fast asleep. With the cloaking ring on, it was easy to stroll out of the house and walk to the cabin where Noah lived with the Southern Vale pack.

I didn't have a chance to knock before Noah yanked the door open, staring down at me with eyes that held so many loving emotions that it was impossible to separate one from the next, and pulled me into a passionate kiss. This kiss was everything I'd *wanted* with him at so many times during the day, when we'd kept ourselves in check because of being surrounded by others. Now, we could truly be together without holding back.

I wanted him—*all* of him—and I was ready for this.

Sometime during the kiss, he picked me up and carried me into his bedroom. The master bedroom, since he was the alpha of the pack.

"How did you know I was there?" I asked, staring up into his eyes as he lowered me onto the bed.

"The imprint bond," he said, and I realized of course —even with my cloaking ring on, he could sense me through the bond. "I haven't been able to sleep all night," he continued. "Everything you feel... everything you want... I want it to. You have no idea how much." His eyes swirled with emotion, and I *did* have an idea how much he wanted this. Because I felt the same way.

"You're ready to mate?" I felt insanely vulnerable as I watched his face for his reaction.

Luckily, all I saw was love and, more surprisingly, relief.

"I've wanted to mate with you since the first time I kissed you in New Orleans," he said. "Hell, I wanted you before that. But the imprinting caught me off guard. If we hadn't been in public when we imprinted, I think I would have taken you as my mate right then and there."

My cheeks heated. Because I had a feeling that if that had been the situation, I would have let him have his way with me, even though I'd never been with anyone like that before.

"You and I are meant for each other, Raven," he continued. "We always have been, and we always will be." He paused and pulled back, worried. "But are *you* ready? You're the one who said you wanted your mom

11

to be there..." He let the sentence trail off, waiting for me to make my decision.

"I'm ready." Every inch of my body pulsed with desire for him, making it nearly impossible to focus on thinking clearly. "It's the twenty-first century. We can mate now, and have the official ceremony later—once my mom is here and can celebrate with us. But this— right here, right now—feels right. I don't want to go into the Trials tomorrow without truly being with you. I love you. You're the only man I've ever loved, and the only man I *will* ever love. So yes, I'm more than ready for us to mate." I pulled him in for a kiss, and his lips slammed into mine, an unspoken agreement that he felt the same way.

Until this moment, whenever we'd been together it had been controlled—careful.

Now, that caution was abandoned as we used our hands to explore every inch of each other. I was lost in everything about Noah—his taste, his feel, his scent. I could feel how much he wanted me, as he could feel the same in return.

Before long all of our clothes were off, leaving us only in our underwear. And I'd never felt more ready for anything in my life.

But just as his hands moved around my back to unhook my bra clasp, his bedroom door flew open, slamming against the wall behind it. My breath caught in my chest, and we both turned to see who was daring to intrude on such an intimate moment.

Sarah—the eldest wolf in the pack—stood in the arch of the doorway. Her eyes were lowered, and her cheeks were flushed red in embarrassment.

I would have assumed the intrusion was an accident… but she had supernaturally strong hearing. She knew exactly what she was walking in on.

"I'm sorry," she said, still not meeting either of our eyes. "But as the eldest member of the pack, it was my duty to stop you from continuing."

"You want to stop me from claiming my mate?" Noah growled, not moving from where he hovered protectively above me.

I'd never considered myself the type of person who would want to be "claimed," but wow, it sounded hot when he said it.

"I'm stopping you from risking Raven's chance in the Angel Trials tomorrow," Sarah said, more confidently now as she raised her gaze to ours.

Silence filled the room. That was a surefire way to kill the mood.

"What do you mean by that?" I moved out from under Noah's body, and the two of us sat up. We were still both in our underwear, but Sarah wasn't flustered.

Which made sense, since shifters weren't as modest as humans.

"To enter the Angel Trials and drink from the Holy Grail, you need to be human." Sarah's wise eyes focused on me. "But when shifters mate, our souls link for all eternity. That's how dyads are created."

I nodded, since I knew about dyads. I'd seen one when I'd first joined Noah's hunt. The shifter who could shift into the forms of both a coyote and a mountain lion.

Dyads were only created in the rare circumstance when two shifters with different animal forms imprinted on and mated with each other.

"Hold on." I held a hand up to my forehead, taking this all in. "You think that when Noah and I mate, I'll become a shifter?"

"I have no idea what will happen when the two of you mate, since a shifter has never mated with a human," she said, moving closer to us. "No one knows what will happen to you. So is right now—the night before the most important day of your human life—the proper time to conduct this experiment?"

When she said it like that, I felt like an idiot. Judging by Noah's silence, he felt the same way.

"I just couldn't imagine going into the Trials tomorrow without us mating first." I wrapped my arms around myself, swallowing as I prepared to say the rest of what I'd been thinking. "Because what if I don't make it tomorrow?"

"If you don't make it tomorrow, then you'll have mated with Noah, and you'll have stopped him from ever finding a possible mate again," she said, her words cutting deep. "Shifters mate once, and it's for life. You know that."

I took a sharp breath inward. Because in my anxious, exhausted, scared, lust-crazed mind, I couldn't bear the thought of dying tomorrow without mating with Noah.

How had I forgotten the most important part—that if we mated and I didn't survive the Trials, he'd never find true love again?

I glanced over at Noah. From the angry way he was staring at Sarah, he was pissed at her for bringing it up.

I shook my head in horror at myself for almost having gone through with it without thinking about every possible outcome. "You should have said something," I told him. "You should have reminded me."

"There was no need." He faced me, his eyes hard. "Because first of all, you're going to survive tomorrow. I have no doubt about it. Secondly, I'll never love anyone as much as I love you, imprint bond or no. I meant what I said earlier. You've always been the one for me, and you always will be the one for me. That's never chang-ing. Ever."

"I know that," I said, because I did. "And you're always going to be the one for me. But Sarah's right."

The older woman crossed her arms and grinned. "I usually am," she said.

I rolled my eyes at her, and refocused on Noah. "I love you," I said. "And even though I'm worried about tomorrow, I *do* believe I can do this. But in the chance that I don't make it, I want you to be able to find love again." He moved his mouth to speak, but I continued before he could. "And what if Sarah's right, and mating changes me into something not human?" I asked. "I've worked so hard for all these months. So many people are counting on me to pass these Trials. It would be selfish of us to do anything to risk that from happening."

Noah's eyes flared with a range of emotions. But because of his silence, I could tell he was coming around to seeing the point.

"Fine," he said after a few tense seconds. "But we're mating after you pass those Trials and become a Nephilim."

"Deal." Heat rushed through my body as I stared longingly into his eyes.

"And you're sleeping here tonight."

Sarah inched out of the room so she stood in the

doorway again. "Now that I've helped the two of you come to your senses, I'm seeing myself out," she said, looking at us in amusement. "Your sleeping arrangements are none of my business. And Raven? Go kick ass in those Trials tomorrow. We're all rooting for you."

"Thanks." I gave her a small smile before she left and closed the door, leaving Noah and me alone again.

I turned my gaze up to meet his and bit my lip. "Are you sure sleeping in the same room is a smart idea?" I asked, glancing at both of our nearly naked bodies.

Yes, we'd slept in the same bed before. But we'd never let things get so heated between us. Now that we had—now that I'd finally let myself *want* him instead of forcing myself to hold back my desire—I wasn't sure I could return to the way things had always been before tonight.

Plus, Darra would throw a fit if I didn't sleep in the manor house with the rest of the students.

"You might not be able to control yourself around me, but I'm more than practiced in controlling myself around you." He smirked, some of his shaggy brown hair falling over his forehead. "And if you want to do your best in the Trials tomorrow, you need sleep. You were so busy thinking about me that you weren't getting any sleep in your room at the academy. There's only one way to fix that. You sleep here, with me."

I stared at him, knowing he'd won me over before he was done speaking. "You're impossible to resist," I said. "You know that?"

"Of course I know that." He smirked again, as confident as ever. Then he found our pajamas strewn across the bed and floor, and handed me mine. "But since we'll just be sleeping, you need to put these back on," he said. "It's best not to tempt the wolf."

"Wolves aren't the only ones who can be tempted." I allowed my eyes to roam across his perfectly tan, fit body, even though I knew I was only torturing myself further by doing so.

My self-imposed torture unfortunately didn't last long, because he put his pajamas back on, and I did the same.

"Good night, Raven," he said, pulling me under the covers with him and snuggling me into his body. We fit together perfectly—like we were made for each other. "I love you."

"I love you too," I repeated, and then in his arms, I finally fell asleep.

4

RAVEN

NOAH WALKED me back to the manor house the next morning, waiting in the hall as I freshened up and changed into my black academy jumpsuit.

I stared at myself in the mirror before leaving. I was the same person I'd been when I'd arrived here, but also not. Toned muscles lined my body where it had been soft before, and I was more confident than ever. After a rocky first few days, the people of Avalon had accepted me and I'd quickly found my place here. In the past three months, this island had become my home.

I couldn't wait to bring my mom and Sage here. They'd love it just as much as I did.

I also couldn't stop myself from thinking that this was what I would be wearing when I either became the first human to drink from the Holy Grail and become a Nephilim, or when I died. Hopefully the former.

Anxiety and excitement shot through my body. It seemed like just yesterday that I'd first stepped foot in the academy. Now that the Big Day was finally here, I felt ready, but also not. I didn't think this was the sort of thing anyone ever felt fully prepared for.

Not wanting to get caught in a loop of worrying about how the day would pan out, I rejoined Noah outside. He took my hand in his, sending confidence through the imprint bond that helped calm down my nerves. I gave him a nod of thanks, and together, we walked down the steps and into the dining hall.

Darra stared us down like a hawk as we entered. "Sleep well last night?" she asked as we took our normal seats by the far window.

"Very well, thank you," I said as I poured myself a glass of Holy Water. "You?"

"Same." From the way she was looking at Noah and me, I could tell she knew exactly where I'd been last night.

Luckily, she didn't say a word about it as we ate breakfast. And unlike the night before, people were giving me my space again. It was like they could feel the nervousness buzzing from my skin, and were afraid of getting too close.

After breakfast, we left the manor house and were greeted by our unicorns and wyverns, as always. But unlike always, our magical creatures didn't take us to our training grounds.

Today, they took us to the arena where I'd compete in the next Trial.

The obstacle course looked like something straight out of that Ninja Warrior television show. I'd seen the course many times, since I'd been practicing on it. It was built entirely on top of a lake, so the water could cushion any falls. During practices—especially in the early weeks—I'd fallen into that water more times than I cared to admit.

The obstacle course didn't intimidate me anymore.

The bleachers packed with every citizen of Avalon, on the other hand, did.

Annar trotted us over to the designated "waiting area"—a space resembling a dugout outside the arena. The Earth Angel Annika was already there when Noah, Darra, and I arrived. Another glance at the arena showed me that her fiancé Jacen was already seated in the center box, along with the three mages Dahlia, Violet, and Iris. The mages wore bright colored, floor-length gowns, as always. They weren't the types to blend into a crowd.

Annika wore simple jeans with a green blouse, and

she looked bright and confident as she watched us approach. I'd been so busy training over the past three months that I hadn't been able to spend much time with her. But she looked so much happier than she had the day I'd met her, when she'd been depressed and hiding away in her room.

I suspected that had to do with me—well, with her faith that I'd be the first human to survive drinking from the Holy Grail.

I couldn't let her down.

"Raven." She smiled at me when I stepped into the dugout. "How are you feeling?"

"Ready." I hoped that the more I said it, the more it would become true. But as I glanced at the crowd again, my stomach swirled with those annoying nerves.

How had this day come so quickly?

Darra followed my gaze out to the crowd. "Remember—the onlookers are the only thing different about today," she said. "You've successfully completed this course in practice ten times now. You've got this."

"I know." Her words helped, but only slightly. I didn't think I'd feel better until I finished the course, drank from the Grail, and learned my fate once and for all.

"Pretend they're not there," Noah said. "And if it becomes too hard, look for me. I'll be following along on the sideline, with you the entire way."

"As will I," Darra added.

I took a deep breath, imagining it calming me down as it made its way through my body. "Thanks, guys," I said. "I needed that."

Annika watched us all talking, although she was mostly focused on me. "I don't imagine you want to put this off any longer," she said, and I nodded, since it was like she was reading my mind. "Very well." She smiled. "Good luck, and I'll see you at the final platform."

She flashed out, teleporting herself onto the final platform—the one where I'd drink from the Grail.

And then, with Noah on one side and Darra on the other, I raised my chin high and walked to the start of the obstacle course.

5

RAVEN

As I stepped up to the first platform, the crowd erupted into applause. The clapping and yelling thundered in my mind. It was like a physical thing, adding pressure that hadn't been there before. I felt like I was drowning in it.

But then I looked to Noah, who was standing where he said he'd be on the sideline with Darra, and the pressure released. I could breathe again.

I glanced over the crowd once more, refusing to let them interfere with my performance. I could do this. I'd already proven it to myself ten times.

But it was different to prove it in front of others.

When I looked at the main central box again, I saw that Thomas had joined Jacen and the mages. He was seated next to Jacen, and in his formal suit and stiff posture, he looked as intense as ever. I knew why. Sage's future rested on what happened to me after I drank from the Grail. If I couldn't become Nephilim, she could be lost to him forever.

Determination burst through me. I needed to succeed. I refused to let down the people I loved.

I glanced at Annika to begin, and the Earth Angel raised her arms, silencing the crowd. Her golden eyes shined under the light of the sun, and she looked every bit an angel.

"Welcome to Raven Danvers's second Trial." Either the acoustics of the arena carried Annika's voice through the entire space, or she was using magic to amplify it. "Raven will have fifteen minutes to complete all of the obstacles in the course. If she succeeds, she'll immediately progress to the third Trial—drinking from the Holy Grail to transform her blood from that of a human to that of a Nephilim. If her body accepts the transition, she'll move onto the final Trial to ignite her powers." She glanced to me, gave me a nod of confidence, and turned to face the mages. "Now… it's time to begin."

On her cue, the mages all stepped forward to stand at the front of the main box and raised their hands to the sky. Colorful streams of magic burst out of each of their palms. Red from Dahlia's, purple from Violet's, and green from Iris's. Their magic matched the colors of the dresses they always wore. The magic swirled together above the obstacle course, coming together to form a giant, luminescent timer in the sky.

It reminded me of the magical timers from the simulation during King Arthur's challenges.

The fifteen minutes started counting down, and I was off.

Darra's training immediately kicked into gear. Don't pay attention to the timer. Don't pay attention to the crowd. The obstacle I was trying to complete was all that mattered.

The first obstacle was the boulder run. I'd completed it the first time I'd done this course, and back then it had been challenging. Now it was a breeze. I jumped from boulder to boulder, arriving at the next platform like I'd been born for this.

Next was the log drop. This had been where I'd fallen into the water the first time I'd tried completing the course. But back then, I'd had no training.

Now, I held tightly onto the log as it slid down the zip line, prepared for both times when it suddenly dropped in an attempt to knock me off. I held on firmly, landing on the opposing platform with ease. I didn't pause before running toward the next obstacle—the floor that rotated under my feet—and zipped across it without stumbling or falling off.

The first three obstacles were down, and faster than ever. I had this.

Next was the big swing that launched me into a roped net, which I needed to climb down toward the next platform. This was one of my favorites during practices. I'd always loved swings.

I jumped up onto the swing, using my bodyweight to gain momentum. I swung once, twice, three times. On the fourth time, I launched myself onto the netted ropes.

As I was flying through the air, someone in the crowd screamed, "You're running to your death!"

My breath caught in my chest. Time froze around me. I stopped thinking for a second—and that one second was enough that my right hand slipped off of the line of rope I was aiming for, my feet missing it entirely.

I was supposed to have landed on the rope holding onto it with both my hands *and* feet. Now I dangled from it with only my non-dominant hand. I was slipping by the second.

If I fell into the water below, the Trial would be over.

I refused to let one jerk in the crowd mess this up for me. So, using the strong muscle I now had in my body thanks to weeks of training, I swung my body forward and got myself situated firmly in the rope net. I began the climb down, keeping my hands and feet gripped firmly as I got closer and closer to the next platform.

Once I was close enough, I jumped onto the platform, landing solidly on my feet.

I took a breath to compose myself, and glanced to where Noah and Darra were following my path on the sideline.

Noah clapped, staring up at me with fire in his eyes. "You can do this!" he said.

I nodded in acknowledgment. Because he was right. I *could* do this.

It didn't matter what a jerk in the crowd thought. I'd complete this course, and then I'd become the first human to drink from the Grail and survive.

I couldn't wait to prove my doubters and haters wrong.

From that point forward, I attacked every obstacle just like Darra had taught me in training. I drowned out the crowd—well, I drowned out everything but Noah and Darra's encouragement.

Pride shined in their eyes with every obstacle I completed. I was so lucky to have them in my life. I wasn't going to let a day go by without telling them that.

When I reached the warped wall—a nearly vertical wall about three times my height—I stared up at it, focusing and preparing. This was the second hardest obstacle in the course.

Which was exactly why Darra had trained me with it

extensively. I'd done my fair share of falling on my face with this one, especially in the early weeks. I definitely didn't want to do that in front of the crowd, even though I could technically keep trying until the timer ran out. I wanted to get it on my first try. The key was not to get intimidated, so my mind wouldn't hold me back.

I rocked back and forth on my heels a few times, and then ran up at it in full force. My momentum carried me far up enough that I was able to grip the flat top of the wall and pull myself up. Those torturous pull-ups I'd been forced to do at the gym were really coming in handy now.

The crowd went crazy when I pulled myself up onto the top platform, successfully completing the warped wall. But I didn't pause to congratulate myself. Because there were more obstacles ahead, and none of what I'd done so far mattered if I didn't finish those in time.

As I continued on and got closer to the final, most difficult obstacle of the course, the crowd clapped louder and louder. There were no more discouraging comments—or at least, there were so many encouraging ones that they drowned out anything else. And anyway, I focused on Noah and Darra's cheers. Those were the ones that mattered the most.

After swinging and leaping from poles like Tarzan, I

reached the final obstacle of the course. The spider climb. A tall, chimney-like structure with the front wall missing.

All I had left was to jump inside and scale it up to reach the top platform where Annika was waiting.

When Darra had first demonstrated the course to me, she'd made every obstacle look easy, including this one. And sure, the course was easy—for a vampire. Not so much for a human.

I stared at the spider-climb and pressed my hands together, preparing myself. Once I started, I couldn't stop or I'd risk losing energy and momentum. Like the other obstacles, I just had to go for it.

I glanced at Noah and Darra, and both of them stared back at me confidently. I could feel their thoughts in their heavy stares. They knew I could do this.

Physically, they were right. I could do it—I'd done it before in practices. Mentally was a different story. Because this wasn't a practice session.

Now the Holy Grail, AKA my possible death, waited for me at that final platform.

Terror rushed my veins at the thought. But then I saw Thomas in the box again, noticing the steady way he was watching on me, depending on me. The weight of responsibility pressed on my chest. Because my mom's life, Sage's life, and countless other lives… they all depended on these next few moments.

I refused to forget that.

I also didn't come this far to wimp out now.

And so, I braced myself at the bottom of the vertical space, positioning myself so both my hands and feet were on the sides of the wall. Then I launched myself up to hold onto the area directly above. Again, and again, and again, and again. I launched myself ten times.

Before I knew it, I was at the top of the spider climb, pulling myself up to join Annika at the final platform where she waited with the Holy Grail.

6

RAVEN

THE TIMER UP above burst into fireworks the moment my feet hit the platform. The flairs of red, purple, and green magic lit up the sky, celebrating my victory.

But all I could focus on was the Holy Grail.

The large, intricately designed chalice sat on a small table next to Annika. It was an intense shade of gold, so bright that the sunlight reflected off it strongly enough to nearly burn my eyes. It was beautiful, but in a scary, intimidating way.

The firework show ended, and the crowd was silent. They'd been cheering and talking for the entire time before now, so the silence felt strange. Heavy.

Noah and Darra had already joined Jacen, Thomas, and the mages in the center box. I would have loved for Noah to be standing on the platform with me right now.

Weeks ago, I'd asked Annika if it would be possible. But because of strict protocol, it wasn't allowed. The only person I was supposed to be close to during the ceremony was the Earth Angel.

And as much as I wanted Noah by my side during this moment, I didn't want to test fate. This was my Trial, and mine alone. Once I drank from the Grail and survived, I would go right back to his side.

And once I ignited my powers and become Nephilim, the two of us would finally be able to mate. Fire burned through my belly as I looked into Noah's soulful brown eyes. He might not be physically close to me right now, but he was still there, watching every moment.

I knew it was going to be like this. I'd been prepared.

But at the same time, I yearned to reach for his hand so he could assure me it was going to be okay.

He did the best thing he could in the circumstance. He sent a surge of strength, confidence, and most importantly, *love* through the imprint bond. The emotions warmed my soul, reminding me that I was strong and ready for this.

Well, as ready to potentially face my death as anyone could be. Because I couldn't deny that there was a part of myself that was scared. No—I was terrified. But I pushed that feeling down, forcing it away with the knowledge that what I was about to do would give me the power to save my loved ones, and the world.

"Congratulations on completing your second Angel Trial." Annika's sharp voice pulled me back to the present. She was staring at me, her golden eyes that matched the Grail shining with a mix of hope and concern. "Now, it's time for your third Trial. Drinking from the Holy Grail."

She stepped up to the Grail and pulled a dagger out of her weapons belt. It was a gorgeous, steel dagger with a large green gemstone at the bottom of the handle—a jade. I recognized the crystal from my time working at Tarotology. It mainly represented luck and strength, but it also fostered courage and love.

Those were all things I needed right now.

Annika held the dagger above the inside of her wrist. She took a deep breath, and then slid the tip of the weapon in a straight, clean line across her skin. From the way she pressed her lips together, I guessed it hurt her as much as it would hurt anyone. But she was doing a good job at hiding it.

The gash slit open, revealing golden blood underneath. Her blood was the same color as her eyes. I never thought of blood as something that could be beautiful. But hers was.

She flipped her wrist over and allowed the golden

liquid to flow into the Grail, like some sort of holy waterfall. She must have allowed at least a pint to spill inside before she pulled her wrist back toward herself. When she did, the gash healed, leaving her porcelain skin flawless once again.

"Whenever you're ready," she said. "Lift the Grail, and drink the entirety of the contents inside."

Everyone in the crowd stared at me. It was like they'd all stopped breathing at once. Their fear rippled out toward me, feeling like it might crush me where I stood.

But then my eyes found Noah's. And just like that, the crowd didn't matter anymore. It was just Noah, the Earth Angel, and the Holy Grail.

I reached for the Grail and picked it up. It was heavier than I'd expected. Probably because it was solid gold. But I didn't falter, thanks to the muscles I'd developed during all those weeks of training.

Staring into its contents, it struck me for the first time that I'd be drinking blood. Weird. At least Annika's blood was gold instead of red, so it didn't *look* like blood. It literally looked like melted gold. At least that made it slightly less strange.

I lifted the Grail closer to my face and took a deep breath in. Her blood smelled sweet—like honeysuckle and nectar. My mouth watered at the delicious scent.

Something about it called to me. Like it was begging me to try it.

Unable to resist the blood, I held the rim of the Grail to my lips, tipped it upward, and drank.

The angel blood exploded in a delicious burst on my tongue. No fruit in the world could compete with such a perfect flavor. It was like it ignited every one of my taste buds at once. Incredible.

I drank and drank and drank, chugging it down until there was no more blood left in the Grail. At least I didn't think there was any more. I tilted it nearly vertically to get the final drops, not wanting to miss a bit.

If this blood was going to be a poison that ended my life, at least it tasted divine.

When there was no more blood left, I lowered the Grail, licking the last of the delicious liquid from my lips.

The crowd stared at me, shocked silent.

They were waiting for me to die.

7

RAVEN

NOTHING HAPPENED.

My stomach felt full, like I'd just had a large meal. But that was the only change I noticed.

"Well?" I looked to Annika nervously. "What's next?"

"You did it." She spoke quietly, but with everyone so silent, her voice filled the arena. "Your body accepted my blood."

"But I feel the same as I did before." I still held onto the Grail, hugging it close to my body. "How can you know it worked?"

"The others died after their first few sips." She gazed out to the hilltops in the distance, as if remembering them. Then she refocused on me. "They could barely force any of my blood down before it killed them."

"Oh." I shifted awkwardly from side to side. "Well, I

definitely didn't have to force it down. Your blood tasted amazing."

Annika chuckled at that. There were laughs in the crowd, too. "Thank you," she said. Then she glanced at Jacen with heat in her eyes, and I had a feeling I wasn't the only person in this arena who'd had a taste of her blood. But I guessed that was normal when your fiancé was a vampire.

"But I don't feel different," I repeated. "Shouldn't your blood have turned me into a Nephilim?"

"You now have Nephilim blood," she reminded me. "But you still haven't ignited your powers. You won't feel any differently until you do."

"How do you know?" I asked.

"I was born Nephilim, but I thought I was human until I made my first supernatural kill," she answered. "Not even supernaturals could sense the difference in me. It's what kept young, not ignited Nephilim children safe, back before we nearly went extinct."

I nodded, her statement reminding me that even though I'd survived drinking from the Grail, my journey was far from over. So I placed the Grail back onto the stand.

As I did, the crowd rose to their feet, clapping and cheering. Noah, Thomas, and Jacen were the first three up.

My cheeks heated at the realization that they were cheering for me.

Because I'd done it.

I'd drunk angel blood from the Holy Grail and survived. It felt unreal. But I'd really, truly done it.

Suddenly, the ground started to rumble and shake. At first it was only a bit, but it got more and more intense.

An earthquake.

I dropped to the floor and gripped the rail of the platform. When I looked at Noah, I saw he'd also dropped to the ground and was holding onto the rail of the box.

Others in the stands were trying to run out in panic, although they were falling down, since the ground was shaking like crazy.

Idiots. Earthquake 101 taught that when a quake started, you needed to drop down, hold on, and wait it out. Growing up in California, it was practically drilled into my head as a kid.

The shaking got stronger, although by some miracle, none of the surrounding structures were breaking. Even the Holy Grail stayed centered on the table, exactly where I'd placed it down. It had to be magic. That seemed to be the only explanation for all strange happenings on Avalon.

Then, out of the corner of my eye, I saw something appear from the center of the lake beside the obstacle course. I turned my head fully to check it out, awed at what I was seeing.

It was the tip of a mountain. The water rippled around it, flowing down the sides of the mountain as it rose. It soon grew into a full mountain that took up the majority of what remained of the lake. The shiny brown, ridged surface of the dirt looked like it had been under-water for centuries.

Once the mountain emerged, the shaking stopped.

I stared at the mysterious mountain in wonder. Because the fact that a mountain had just risen out of the lake wasn't the strangest thing I saw before me.

The strangest thing was the moss-covered boulder in the center with a glimmering golden sword hilt sticking out of the top.

8

RAVEN

NOAH, Jacen, and the mages joined Annika and me on the platform. The supernaturals were able to scale the chimney climb way faster and easier than I had, making the obstacle look like a piece of cake.

"Are you okay?" Noah looked down at me in concern, studying every inch of my body to make sure I wasn't injured.

"I'm fine." I moved toward him and wrapped him in a hug, thrilled to just be alive. "I'm more than fine," I said once I pulled away, staring up into his eyes in amazement. "I survived drinking from the Grail."

"I knew you would." He smirked.

"Really?" I raised an eyebrow in challenge. "Because you seemed worried beforehand too…"

"I'll always worry about you." He placed his hands on

my hips, holding me strong and steady. "I love you. But worrying about you doesn't mean I don't believe in you. It just means I care about you. Always."

"Thanks." I beamed. "Right back at you."

He pulled me into a short kiss, although it ended quickly, as he turned his attention to the mountain that had just risen from the sea. Then he looked to the mages. "What do you make of this?" he asked them.

"It appears to be the sword in the stone," Iris said.

"Not just *any* sword," Dahlia added. "The Holy Sword."

"Excalibur," Violet finished up. "King Arthur's sword itself."

The three sisters gazed at the mountain in disbelief. I also studied the hilt of the sword embedded into the stone. Now that they'd mentioned it, I noticed it was the same shade of gold as the Holy Grail.

Iris cleared her throat and faced the questioning crowd. They looked shaken after the earthquake, but supernaturals healed quickly. No one was gravely injured. "Citizens of Avalon!" She raised her hands, a burst of green magic shimmering around her palms, and everyone went silent. "After Raven survived drinking the Earth Angel's blood from the Holy Grail, we received a sign from King Arthur. He has gifted us with his Holy Sword Excalibur, which has been missing since his generation of Nephilim defeated the demons centuries ago. But like it was when he first stumbled upon it, Excalibur is embedded into a stone. Only the one worthy of the Holy Sword will be able to free it and claim it as his or her own." She spoke like she'd expected this, although from the way she'd gazed up at the mountain a minute before, I knew she was as surprised as the rest of us.

Enthusiastic chattering filled the crowd. All the terror from earlier was gone. The earthquake was forgotten now that something more exciting was happening.

Had I caused this? After all, the mountain had only risen after I'd survived drinking from the Grail. It had to be connected.

Jacen took Annika's hand and stepped forward. "I can think of no one better to try freeing the sword than our leader of Avalon, the Earth Angel," he said, sneaking a glance at Annika. "If that's what she wants, of course."

The crowd cheered, apparently in agreement with that plan.

"I'm more than happy to try," she said once they'd quieted enough so she could speak.

They cheered again, which appeared to please her.

In a flash, she teleported from where she was standing with us on the platform and onto the top of the newly raised mountain. She wrapped her hands around the golden handle of the sword and pulled.

It didn't budge.

She braced herself and pulled harder, putting her entire body into it. But no matter how hard she pulled, the sword stayed where it was.

Finally, she let go of the handle and turned back around to face the group of us on the platform. "Raven," she said, her golden eyes focused on me. "The mountain didn't rise from the lake until after you survived drinking from the Grail. I don't think it rose for me. I think it rose for you. So you should be the one to try freeing the sword from the stone."

I nodded, since it was the same thing I'd thought earlier. But unfortunately, I couldn't teleport to the top of the mountain like Annika had done. I wouldn't be able to do that even after igniting my Nephilim power, since teleporting was limited to angels, greater demons, witches, and mages.

Which meant I needed to climb the mountain myself. It wasn't what I'd planned on doing after completing the challenging obstacle course and drinking from the Grail. But luckily, my training had prepared me for situations like this.

Annika teleported back over to my side. "Want me to bring you to the top of the mountain?" she asked, holding a hand out to me. "You've more than proven your capabilities today. There's no need to exert yourself further."

I glanced at the top of the mountain where the sword in the stone waited, to her hand, and back again. "Thanks," I said, keeping my hands by my sides. "But if you're right that this mountain rose for me, I want to get to the top on my own."

"Very well." She nodded, and I swore I saw respect in her eyes. "Go get that sword."

The crowd cheered again and started chanting my name over and over, until it sounded like a song of its own. I suspected this might have been the most exciting thing to happen on Avalon since, well… since Annika and Jacen had arrived and claimed the island as theirs.

The climb down from the top platform was easier than the way up, since I was able to take the ladder. Once I was back at the lower platform, I eyed up the distance between it and the bottom of the mountain. Only a few feet of water. I could either swim, or jump for it.

I didn't love swimming, and jumping would make a better show. So I backed up as far as possible, got a running start, and leaped from the edge of the platform to the bottom of the mountain.

I landed perfectly on my feet.

The crowd cheered again, and I turned to beam at them. I'd never been the type of person to seek the spotlight. But their energy was so contagious that I couldn't help getting pulled into it.

However, I needed to focus on getting up the mountain. So I turned away from the crowd and studied the possible paths up. Once I picked one, I started to climb. All I had to do was get my hands and feet in the right places. It was challenging, but not as challenging as some of the obstacles I'd just completed on the course. My training had more than prepared me for this.

As I made my way up, I couldn't help thinking about a kids reality show I used to watch when I was younger, where three contestants would race up a glowing mountain called the Aggro Crag. The mountain I was climbing now looked about the same size as the Aggro Crag. It was probably about thirty feet tall—slightly taller than the spider climb.

It didn't take me long to reach the top. Maybe it was the new angel blood running through my veins, but the climb was invigorating. These past few weeks, I'd pushed through training, but I'd never enjoyed it. Now I was loving it.

It *had* to be the angel blood. There no other explanation for my sudden attitude change toward exercising.

Once I reached the top, I came face to face with the sword in the stone. The golden handle gleamed in the sunlight just as intensely as the Holy Grail. The stone was slightly taller than my waist, which put the handle at the perfect height for me to grab.

My body pumped with nervous adrenaline. But there was no time to waste. I was either going to be able to pull the sword from the stone, or I wouldn't be. I might as well stop staring at it and see what happened.

I stepped forward, gripped the handle, and pulled.

The sword slipped free of the stone with no resistance.

As the blade left the rock, red magic surrounded it—just like the sword I'd used in King Arthur's simulation. I raised the beautiful weapon above my head, and the magic swirled around the blade, bright and full of life. My body surged with strength. It was like the magic was traveling from the sword, through my palms, and into my soul.

It felt just as perfect in my hands as it had in the simulation. I gave it a few quick swishes through the air, watching in awe as the magic swirled around the moving blade. It was like this sword and I were meant for each other. Like we'd been separated my whole life, and were finally being reunited.

And this wasn't just any sword. It was Excalibur. The

same sword King Arthur had used to fight off the last of the demons in his time. Incredible.

Before I knew what was happening, Annika and the three mages teleported to my side. They all stared at me with wonder—and with respect.

Annika held the Holy Grail to her side. Now that the Grail and the Sword were so close to each other, it was clear that the gold on them matched exactly. Like they'd been crafted together and made up a pair.

"Raven Danvers," Dahlia said my name, and with her words, the crowd quieted. "King Arthur has chosen you to wield his Holy Sword Excalibur. His weapon belongs to you now. Use it wisely."

"I will," I said, although the weight of the responsibility bore down upon me like bricks. I wasn't sure exactly what I was taking on by being chosen by this sword, but it had to be something big. And judging by the way the sword pulsed with power at the thought, I was right.

"I know you will." Annika smiled at me, and then she turned to Iris. "And I hope there's enough time between now and nightfall for you to plan a party," she said to the mage. "Because tonight, we're celebrating Raven."

9

RAVEN

Iris was truly gifted at quick party planning. Either that, or she'd been planning the party all along, under the assumption that I'd succeed in drinking from the Grail. It was probably the latter, given how incredible the ballroom looked.

Long, wooden banquet tables lined the sides of the room. They were covered with red tablecloths, and lit up candelabras stuffed with azaleas floated magically above. With the tables on the sides, there was space for a dance floor in the center of the ballroom. But the best part was the DJ booth heading up the dance floor. Now that Thomas had used his gift to make technology work on Avalon, the island was no longer stuck in the Dark Ages. Which meant we had access to regular things from Earth, like modern music and a speaker system.

We'd just finished a feast of mana, Holy Water, and wine, and everyone was quick to jump onto the dance floor to continue the party. Bella was owning the DJ booth, playing music and expertly switching from song to song like she was a professional DJ in Miami. Since it was a night for celebration, nearly everyone had indulged in more wine than normal. It was nice to see so many people letting loose and enjoying themselves, since it was usually pretty uptight around here.

But despite joining in and trying to have fun—the celebration *was* for me, after all—it was too soon. I still had to complete the final Trial to activate my Nephilim powers. My mom and Sage's lives were still at risk. I understood why everyone on Avalon wanted to celebrate, since I was the first human who'd successfully drank from the Grail. I was a symbol of hope to them.

But that didn't change the fact that the celebration felt premature to me. Plus, everyone wanted to talk to me and ask me questions. After the day I'd had, it was too much.

So despite all the effort that had gone into planning this party, I already wanted to leave.

"Hey." Noah came up behind me and wrapped his arms around my waist, his soft lips brushing against my ear. "Want to get out of here for a bit?"

"And go where?" I turned to look up at him, smiling

mischievously. It might be too risky to mate before I became a Nephilim, but there were still plenty of other things we could do together alone. And if we only disappeared for a "bit," maybe it wouldn't be too noticeable to the others. They'd all had too much wine to be paying attention to anything for long, anyway.

"A walk," he said. "I thought we could explore the gardens in the courtyard."

I raised an eyebrow. Noah wanted to explore the gardens? Something felt off. He was more of a "run through the wild forest" type of guy. Manicured gardens weren't his thing.

I tried to fish through the imprint bond to feel what was going on, but I got nothing. Whatever was going on, he was purposefully hiding it from me.

Which only made me more curious about what that something was.

"Sure," I said, leading the way off the busy dance floor. "Let's go."

We sneaked out of the ballroom with minimal people noticing. Thomas did, but that was because he wasn't partying. He was sitting in the DJ booth with Bella, a glass of red wine in his hand as he stared blankly out at the blissful crowd.

I didn't blame him. How could he possibly have fun with Sage still living in the Montgomery compound, bound to Azazel?

At least we knew she was alive. If she wasn't, Thomas would have felt the imprint bond break. But I prayed she was doing okay.

Once Noah and I were in the courtyard gardens, I inhaled the flowery air. Now that I was out of the ballroom, I finally felt able to breathe again. We walked along a stone path, arched trees forming an enchanted canopy above our heads. Azaleas in bright colors lined the path, and there were occasional benches and fountains for people to sit and relax. There were lights along the path as well, creating a perfect ambient glow.

A handful of others were walking the gardens as well —mainly couples. Like them, Noah and I walked hand in hand, enjoying the brisk night air and nodding politely at those we passed. Luckily, no one tried to stop and chat. They were also the quieter types, and they seemed to understand that I needed space.

Finally, we reached a circular area with a fountain in the center. Water flowed through the five tiers of the fountain, and each tier was overflowing with flowers, pinecones, vines, and lights. No other people were in sight. It was almost like a spell had been cast around the area for privacy.

"Wow." I gazed upon the fountain, brushing the vines with my fingers. "This is gorgeous."

"I thought you would like it," Noah said.

"You knew this was here?"

"We've been living on Avalon for weeks," he said. "Of course I knew this was here."

"Oh," I said absently. "I guess I've been so busy with training that I haven't had much time to explore."

"You like this spot?" There was something different about the way he was looking at me. He was normally confident and intense, but right now he looked… unsure. Nervous. I wasn't used to seeing him like this.

Hopefully something wasn't wrong.

"I do," I said, and he beamed, his smile making my heart flutter. "It looks like something out of a fairytale."

"Good," he said, and then he did the last thing I expected.

He got down on one knee, reached into his pocket, and removed a black box with a stunning diamond ring inside. The ring was dainty and gorgeous. The diamond was rotated to the side, with bursts of other, smaller diamonds around it, like stars.

My hand went to my lips in shock. Was he proposing? I didn't think that was a thing shifters did.

"Raven Danvers." He cleared his throat, staring up at me with those intense brown eyes I loved so much. "Ever since our first kiss, I've known I wanted to be with you forever. I know I was a bit obtuse in the beginning of our relationship—okay, a lot obtuse—but it was all because I love you. You're the strongest, most stubborn, bravest woman I've ever met. You'll risk anything for the people you love, and I'll risk anything for you. I can't wait for the two of us to mate. But mating is part of shifter culture—not human culture. It's important for us to embrace both of our backgrounds in our union. And so, I'd be honored if you accept my proposal, and agree to become my wife. Once our loved ones are safe and with us on this island, of course."

Sometime during the time he'd been talking, tears had made their way down my cheeks. None of this felt real.

I lowered myself onto the ground to kneel next to him, took his face in my hands, and kissed him. His skin was warm under my touch, and he tasted like earthy cinnamon mixed with a touch of red wine. I didn't think I'd ever be able to get enough of him.

"So." He ended the kiss and rested his forehead against mine. "Is that a yes?"

"Yes." I smiled, blinking away tears. "You already

know I want to mate with you. Of course I want to marry you."

He lifted the ring out of the box and slid it gently onto my finger.

"It's perfect." I touched the delicate rose gold band of the ring, smiling down at it. I didn't think I'd ever be able to stop smiling after tonight. "How'd you know what style I liked?"

"I have my ways." He raised an eyebrow mysteriously. "Also, Thomas offered to hack into something he called your 'Pinterest account.' That helped a lot."

My cheeks flushed. That was so embarrassing. I kept my "dream wedding" Pinterest board secret for a reason, but of course Thomas could hack through that. Oh well. It had resulted in Noah knowing exactly what type of ring I loved, so I couldn't be too angry.

Tonight I'd gone from feeling out of place to feeling happier than ever, and it was all thanks to Noah. Now, I never wanted the night to end.

"Let's stay out here for a while?" I took his hand and led him to the bench that viewed the fairytale fountain.

He sat down next to me. The next thing I knew, his lips were on mine again, and he was kissing me with all of the passion in the world. I could stay here like this with him forever, in this magical garden under the stars.

We'd have to go back inside eventually. But I pushed the thought from my mind.

Because for now, I lost myself in the arms of Noah— the love of my life, my future mate, and as of the past few minutes, my fiancé.

10

RAVEN

My training with Darra resumed for the next few days, as the witches of Avalon prepared the satellite island for my final Trial. Whatever supernatural they chose for me to kill to ignite my powers couldn't get to the actual island of Avalon, since he or she couldn't pass King Arthur's simulation. So the final Trial would happen on a nearby island that was equally as hidden as Avalon.

Until the island was ready, Darra helped me practice using Excalibur. She'd always told me I was a natural with a blade. But now that I had Excalibur, it was like the Holy Sword and I shared a soul. It was like the blade communicated with me, guiding me through each motion. I could finally hold my own in a practice session with Darra. And that was saying a lot, since she was a vampire princess and I was a Nephilim with dormant supernatural abilities.

"Give it all you've got," I challenged as we circled each other like hawks.

"Are you sure about that?" She smirked and raised an eyebrow, holding her own sword up in preparation.

"I'm sure."

She nodded, and then was moving faster than humanly possible. Excalibur helped me defend against her blade for a minute or so. But after that, I couldn't keep up with her supernatural speed and strength. Even *with* the help of the Holy Sword, I soon found myself weaponless, with her blade pressed up against my neck.

"Impressive," she said, lowering her weapon. "I didn't expect you to hold your own for even half that long."

"Yes," someone said from the doorway. "Very impressive."

I turned to see who was there. Camelia. The witch wore a long black maternity gown that covered her pregnant stomach. Her baby bump had grown considerably these past few months. It was now obvious she was pregnant, instead of it looking like she'd possibly eaten too much at dinner. Especially because the rest of her remained perfectly thin.

I supposed that was what happened when a pregnant woman was living on mana and Holy Water. The mana was able to satisfy her every pregnancy craving, while still giving her body the perfect balance of nutrients it needed. So she hadn't gained weight anywhere except the baby bump on her stomach. It was like those Barbie dolls where you popped the bump on their stomach, and that was it.

"What're you doing here?" I asked, although I had my suspicions. The witches didn't venture to the academy grounds unless there was a reason. And there was only one reason Camelia would be seeking me out right now.

"The satellite island is ready," she said. "It's time for you to come with me and learn which supernatural has been selected for you to kill for your final Trial."

11

RAVEN

CAMELIA WALKED me to her private quarters in the castle. She had a full suite with a living room, bedroom, and bathroom. The plush medieval decoration inside was fit for a queen.

"Have a seat." She motioned to the table in the living room. There was a tea party waiting for us, with a three tiered stand holding pieces of white mana and a porcelain teapot sitting on the table.

I took my seat, and she poured each of us a cup of tea. After living on Avalon for three months, I knew the tea had been brewed with Holy Water. I added a bit of creamer and two cubes of sugar, so the tea was exactly how I liked it.

Camelia kept her tea black.

"The supernatural you've been selected to kill is

someone you've already met before," she started, jumping straight to the point. "A male witch named Dr. Foster."

I nearly choked on my tea when she said his name. But I caught myself at the last second and placed the teacup down on the saucer, dabbing the sides of my lips with my napkin. "I thought Dr. Foster was being kept in the prison at the Vale?" I asked.

"He was interrogated at the Vale." Camelia smiled smugly. "There, he confessed to working with the demons to strengthen up gifted humans."

"I know that," I said. "That's what he was doing with us at the bunker."

"Don't you want to know *why* you were being strengthened up?" She leaned forward, like she was taunting me with a secret. No—that was *exactly* what she was doing, and she knew it.

Camelia was enjoying taunting me.

"Judging from what happened to Jessica, it looks like the demons wanted to turn us into vampires," I said, unwilling to give into whatever game Camelia was trying to play.

"That was what we initially thought, too," she said. "But we leaned more from Dr. Foster. Once the gifted humans are turned into vampires, the demons are having them killed and drained of their blood. Therefore, Dr. Foster is a willing accomplice in countless murders. He's been sentenced to death by the rulers of the Vale."

"Hold on." I raised a hand to stop her from saying any more, replaying what she'd told me about what Dr. Foster was doing. "Are you saying that all the gifted humans who were taken from the bunker were turned into vampires and murdered?"

The implication of what that meant for my mom chilled me to the bone. Rosella had promised my mom was alive.

But what if Rosella had been wrong?

"According to Dr. Foster, they were all turned into vampires," she said. "Then, all but two of them were killed."

"Which two?" I leaned forward, praying for the best.

"Your mom and Jessica."

I breathed out a sigh of relief. My mom was alive. She was a vampire… but she was alive.

If it were true that she was a vampire, I was glad of it. She'd be able to hold her own against the demons much better as a vampire than as a gifted human.

"Dr. Foster was under truth potion when he was interrogated," Camelia continued. "He confessed that your mom was kept alive because her heightened vampire ability was more useful to the demons than her slaughtered vampire blood."

Whatever her heightened ability was, I thanked the stars that it had kept her alive. I couldn't wait to see her again so we could catch each other up on everything we'd been through since the night of my birthday. We were so close to reuniting that I could practically taste it.

"What do the demons want with slaughtered vampire blood?" I asked, able to focus more on what Camelia was telling me now that I had confirmation my mom was alive.

"We don't know," she said. "Dr. Foster made a blood oath that he wouldn't tell, so not even our best truth potion can get that information from him. He's told us all he can. Now, it's time for him to face his fate in your final Trial."

RAVEN

I TWISTED my hands in my lap, uncomfortable with this entire thing. "I met Dr. Foster at the bunker," I said, recalling the scared old man who had examined me and put me through a few days of training. He didn't seem like he could hurt a fly. In fact, he'd seemed as helpless against the demons as the rest of us. "I know he was helping the demons. But is it fair for him to be sentenced to death, when he never actually killed anyone himself?"

Camelia took a delicate sip of her tea, and then placed the cup down on the saucer. Her hard eyes didn't leave mine the entire time. The silence between us was tense and uncomfortable.

I didn't move as I waited for her to answer.

"The Kingdom of the Vale has approved Dr. Foster's

sentence," she said. "The kingdoms uphold the law for the entire supernatural society. It's not up to anyone—especially a Nephilim who has yet to come into her powers—to question their decisions."

"I'll question anything I want to question." I held my chin up, refusing to let her intimidate me.

She continued to hold my gaze, not saying anything as she waited for me to back down.

I held my ground.

"Dr. Foster is going to die one way or another," she finally said. "It might as well be by your blade. Especially since male witches are the weakest supernaturals. It practically guarantees your success. And isn't that what you want? To complete the Angel Trials so you can rescue your mom and your shifter friend?"

"Yes, it's what I want," I said. "But can't you give me someone else to kill for my final Trial? A lower level demon, or someone evil, who deserves it?"

Camelia's lower lip curled in disgust. "The Foster witches are an ancient, dark magic circle," she said. "They've aligned themselves with the demons. *All* Foster witches deserve what's coming to them. This is war, and if you want to prove you're worthy of Nephilim powers, you have to first prove yourself capable of taking a supernatural life."

"I'm capable," I said. "You don't have to give me a

male witch because they're the easiest to kill. I've trained for this. I'm ready."

"Get off your high horse," Camelia shot back at me. "You're killing Dr. Foster. Remember, your precious Dr. Foster had no idea Azazel was going to keep your mom alive. He had her turned into a vampire, assuming he was sending her to her death. Is that really the type of person you want to save?"

"I don't want to save him." I clenched my fingers into fists, digging my nails into my palms. "But I don't want to kill him, either. I think he should live out the rest of his miserable existence rotting away in a jail cell."

"What you think doesn't matter." She rolled her eyes, like I was an insolent child. "Killing Dr. Foster isn't a choice. It's a command. And not even your gift of stubbornness is strong enough to change the mind of the king of the Vale."

I pressed my lips together, anger building in my veins as I looked at Camelia's smug face.

"Do you want to be a part of the Earth Angel's army or not?" she asked.

"Of course I do." I didn't have to think twice about my answer.

"Then you need to learn how to follow commands," she said. "Starting with the one to go to the satellite island for your final Trial and kill Dr. Foster so you can ignite your Nephilim powers. You can either complete your task, or refuse and return to Earth. What'll it be?"

I stared at her, dumbstruck. What kind of choice was that? Rosella had told me I *had* to complete the Angel Trials if I wanted the best chance at saving my mom. So I couldn't refuse and return to Earth. Well, technically I could, since I had free will and could do whatever I wanted. But I wouldn't risk my mom's life. If my mom died because I refused to kill Dr. Foster—who *had* sent her to her death—I'd never forgive myself.

I didn't want Dr. Foster to die. But I wanted my mom back more.

Camelia tilted her head, giving me a closed lipped smile. She knew she had me.

"Fine," I gave in, which made Camelia's eyes light up with mirth. "I'll do it. But I'll be asking Darra to teach me how to kill him as painlessly as possible. If he has to die, I want it to be quick."

"Good." The witch leaned back in her chair. "I look forward to seeing you succeed."

I nodded, since my success wasn't up for debate. I *was* going to succeed.

I hadn't come this far to fail now.

"As the most powerful witch on Avalon, I'll be accompanying you to the satellite island," she continued, her hands resting on her pregnant belly as she spoke.

"You'll also be accompanied by your trainer—Darra—and another supernatural of your choosing. The three of us are there to ensure you stay alive on the island, although we cannot interfere with the Trial itself. I suggest you choose the third supernatural wisely. It can be anyone except the Earth Angel and the three mages, since they're required to remain on Avalon at all times. And you need to make the decision now. So, who will it be?"

"Noah," I said, his name leaving my lips easily. There was no one else in the world I trusted as much as I trusted him.

"I figured as much," she said. "A witch, a vampire, and a shifter will be a highly qualified team to protect you."

I'd chosen Noah because we loved each other and trusted each other—not because a shifter would be a logical addition to the group. But Camelia didn't strike me as someone who understood making a decision based on love and trust. So explaining that to her seemed pointless.

And, since her hands were still on her stomach, I couldn't help being reminded about her condition—mainly, about how it would affect my final Trial.

"Should you really be coming to the satellite island with us?" I asked, motioning to her stomach. "I don't want anything to happen to your baby."

"My baby will be fine," she said. "This pregnancy is making my magic stronger, thanks to the baby. Her magic is heightening mine."

"Her?" I asked. "You know she's a girl?"

"I do." Camelia smiled. "Male witches don't have strong magic. Only a girl could give me a boost like this. And she's going to be a strong one. I can feel it." She moved her hands from her stomach and sat straighter, back to business. "Anyway, we've talked about what I brought you in here to discuss. Do you have any more questions?"

"No," I said, since Darra had been preparing me for my Trials in our training sessions. I knew exactly what to expect.

"Good," she said, looking mighty pleased with herself. "Then I'll see you at the final Trial tomorrow."

13

SKYLAR

I WAS WOKEN at sunset by a knock on the door. Mara. I smelled her familiar smoky demon scent—along with a hint of earthy shifter—from here.

My wake up calls at the Montgomery compound had been much more pleasant since Mara had taken over the duty of giving me my twice daily blood and complacent potion.

I stretched and got out of bed. "Come in," I said, walking over to the small table where I'd have my breakfast.

Mara let herself in. As always, she carried a silver platter with her. On it was a glass of blood and a syringe of dark blue complacent potion.

"Your breakfast," she said, placing the glass of blood down on the table in front of me.

"Thank you." My mouth watered at the sweet, warm scent of the blood. But I wrapped a hand around it and forced myself to drink it slowly, savoring it.

When I'd first arrived at the compound, fresh from being turned into a vampire, I hadn't been able to stop myself from downing blood in a few gulps. But in the past few weeks, I'd been practicing control. I could now drink the blood in a civilized manner, instead of like an animal.

I'd made a lot of progress since arriving here.

Mara sat in the seat across from me. "Once you're finished with your breakfast, Azazel wants to see you," she said.

"Another tarot reading," I said, since that was the only reason Azazel *ever* wanted to see me.

"Most likely." Her trusting eyes didn't leave mine. Her demonic red eyes.

It was pretty unbelievable that after all these weeks at the compound, the person I'd gotten closest to was a demon. Even crazier was that Mara had truly grown on me. We'd spent a lot of time together, and she'd become the second daughter I'd never had.

"Very well, then." I raised the glass to my lips again, downing the rest of the blood. Once finished, I placed it back on the table. "I don't want to keep His Grace waiting."

"How considerate of you," Mara said, reaching for the needle on the tray. "We'll finish this up, and then head straight to his office."

I nodded to give her the okay.

And with that, she stood up, prepared the needle filled with complacent potion, and pressed down on the syringe.

Mara led the way out of the guesthouse and toward the main house.

I walked behind her, as always. By walking behind her, I showed the others in the compound that I acknowledged her as the superior species—the species that deserved to be followed and obeyed.

Once inside, she knocked on the doors to Azazel's office. He told us to come in, and she swung them open, walking in first. I followed behind, keeping my eyes to the floor.

Azazel sat in the chair behind his giant desk, leaning back with his legs sprawled out in front of him. "Skylar," he said, grinning at me. "Just the prophetess I wanted to see. You look well."

"She's been so behaved these past few weeks." Mara

smiled at me, like I was a prized pet. "I think she's truly coming around to seeing things our way."

Azazel pressed his lips together and tilted his head, studying me. "Don't be so easily fooled, daughter," he finally said. "She might want us to think she's coming around to our side. But she hasn't. And she won't—at least, not until her daughter joins us."

Every muscle in my body tightened at the mention of Raven.

Azazel was trying to bait me. And I wouldn't let him.

"You want me to do a tarot reading for you?" I jumped to the heart of the matter, since I had no interest in sitting around chit chatting with Azazel.

"I do." He reached inside his leather jacket, pulled out my tarot deck, and placed it on the desk. The box for the cards was falling apart so much that he'd resorted to using a beer koozie to hold it together.

So uncivilized. He needed a tarot case. But what else should I have expected from a demon?

I sat down across from him, removed the koozie from the tarot case, and slid out the cards. They felt warm and alive in my hands. I shuffled them, feeling the energy buzzing from them as I moved them around.

"What do you want to know today?" I asked.

He smirked and leaned forward, resting his arms on

the desk. "Kara has had her first moon bleed," he said, his eyes glinting with excitement.

My stomach dropped to my feet, and I stopped shuffling the cards. This was the day I'd been dreading since learning that Azazel could have Kara safely turned into a vampire after she had her first period.

Because Kara's heightened vampire gift was the tool Azazel needed to locate Avalon.

Azazel studied me, like he expected me to congratulate him.

No way in Hell was that happening.

"I see," I said, keeping my voice as steady as possible. I refused to let him see how frightened I was. "What would you like to know?"

"I want to know the best tactic to destroy Avalon." His red eyes gleamed, and he curled his upper lip back, exposing his pointed yellow teeth.

I hated him.

"All right." I nodded and continued shuffling the cards, since the complacent potion gave me no other option but to follow his commands.

Once the cards hummed in my hands, I placed them down onto the desk and fanned them out. I let my hands linger over them, thinking about what I wanted to know until one of the cards pulled me toward it.

I picked that card out of the fan and placed it face up in front of me.

The Ace of Swords.

The card featured a giant sword with an eagle on the hilt, on a bed of roses, with butterflies fluttering around it. The art on this card was one of my favorites, as was the meaning behind it. Resolving a situation, victory, and new beginnings.

It was what we all needed right now.

As had always started happening since I'd become a vampire and my gift of reading tarot cards had heightened, the image on the card disappeared. It changed into a vision that would answer the question I'd asked the deck.

I watched the vision play out, careful to keep my expression neutral. Once the vision finished, I looked back up to meet Azazel's eyes.

"Well?" he asked, tapping the pads of his fingers against the desk. "What did you see?"

I stared up at him and pressed my lips together. I hated how he bossed me around like a slave. But of course, I spoke anyway.

The complacent potion wouldn't give me a choice.

"You need to go to a satellite island off of Avalon," I said. "Kara will be able to find it. Raven will be on the island for her final Angel Trial. You need to kill her before she becomes a Nephilim, and you need to go there alone to be successful. If you don't do this, Raven will end up being your demise."

I clasped my hand over my mouth, looking down in shame.

"It hurts, doesn't it?" Azazel asked. "Being forced to betray your own daughter?"

"You have no idea," I said darkly, turning my gaze up to meet his again. "I'll do anything to save my daughter's life. Whatever you need me to do... tell me. Just don't hurt her. Please."

"Stop your pathetic begging." He stood up and laughed, hollow and amused. "The cards have spoken. My task is set out for me. There's nothing you can do to save Raven now."

14

RAVEN

THE CITIZENS of Avalon gathered on the ocean shore the next morning. I was the first person to reach the final Angel Trial, and the entire island was buzzing in excitement about my send off. Many people were having picnics on the beach as they waited, as if they didn't have a care in the world. It almost looked normal.

Almost.

Once the sailboat was examined and deemed fit to go, Annika led Noah, Darra, Camelia, and me through the crowd and toward the boat. The three mages followed behind us.

Everyone stood up as we started our way down the beach, clearing a path so we could pass. They lowered their heads in respect as we walked by them. We truly were getting a heroes send off.

We stepped up onto the dock, and Annika continued leading the way toward the boat. Once we reached the end, she stopped to face us, although she focused on me.

"This is where you'll leave for your final Trial," she said. "Once you're finished on the satellite island, Camelia will send a fire message to let us know you're on your way back. We'll be waiting here to greet you upon your return. Good luck, and I'll see you soon."

"Thank you," I said, bowing my head slightly. "For everything."

I started to make my way toward the boat, but Annika spoke again before I could get there.

"Oh, and Raven?" she said, and I turned around, waiting for her to continue. "You're going to make an amazing Nephilim."

The crowd cheered in agreement, and one by one, the four of us stepped onto the sailboat. I went first, then Noah, then Darra, and finally, Camelia.

Once we were all onboard, Annika untied the rope holding the boat to the dock. As we floated away, the mages raised their hands to release bursts of colorful magic toward the sails, sending us off toward the satellite island where I'd kill Dr. Foster and ignite my Nephilim powers.

RAVEN

I THOUGHT the satellite island was going to be close to Avalon.

I was wrong.

Thirty minutes after we'd set sail, there was still no sight of another island anywhere. Just blue ocean all around. I trusted the mages' magic not to lead us astray, but I thought we would have been close by now.

We'd all been sitting in the center of the boat, chatting about what felt like absolutely nothing. If Camelia hadn't been there, then Noah, Darra, and I could have had *real* conversations. But the snooty witch was throwing off the group dynamic. No one wanted to open up around her with anything except banal chitchat, and the strain in the conversation was painfully obvious to all of us, including her.

I wanted to sit in comfortable silence with Noah and enjoy the beautiful scenery, but that wouldn't be fair to Darra. My mentor sat as far as possible away from Camelia. The two of them clearly didn't like each other, and I was the reason they were there at all, which meant it was up to me to keep the peace.

"So," I said, glancing at Camelia once the conversation reached another awkward lull. "When's the baby due?"

"Three months," she said, her hands dropping down to her stomach. She smiled—the only time she seemed truly happy was when she was talking about her baby. Other than that, she had resting bitch face all the time. "I can't wait to meet her."

"What about the father?" I asked. She'd never mentioned him, and I was beyond curious about who he was. "Is he excited to meet her, too?"

Her eyes snapped up to meet mine. They were cold and hard. "Her father is no longer in this world," she said, the sentence clipped and final.

"Oh." I leaned back, startled by her response. "Sorry."

I should have realized that the father might have been dead. Camelia was from the Vale, and there had been a big war there around the time she would have gotten pregnant. I'd just been trying to make conversation, and I hadn't stopped to think. Now I felt rude and insensitive.

I needed to save this conversation, quickly.

"Have you decided what you're going to name her?" I asked.

Camelia studied me, her beady eyes full of disdain. "You can stop the terrible attempts at chitchat," she said. "I'm going to protect you on the satellite island because that's my job, and I need to do my job so I'm allowed to continue living on Avalon. I'll do everything I can to make sure you're safe there. But there's no need for us to pretend we like each other now. So back off, and let's continue the rest of the ride there in peace. Unless you have any *relevant* questions, of course."

"What did I do to you to make you hate me this much?" I doubted she considered the question relevant, but it came out before I could think otherwise.

"It's not you." She smiled, although it was clearly fake. "Don't take it so personally. I just don't really like anyone."

"As much as I hate to agree with her, she's right," Noah said. "Camelia's always been like this." He looked to her, like he was trying to see beneath her icy exterior but failing. "It's a miracle the Earth Angel lets you stay on Avalon after what you did to her in the Vale. I can't think of one other person who would be even half as forgiving as she's been."

"What do you mean?" I asked.

"Back in the Vale, Camelia sold out the Earth Angel," he said, apparently not caring that Camelia was sitting there listening to him talk about her. "Pretty much everyone knows the story by now. It was back when the Earth Angel was disguised as Princess Ana... well, disguised as you. It was before she'd ignited her Nephilim powers. Camelia ordered Annika to the throne room and injected her with the antidote to the transformation potion to reveal her true identity in front of Laila—the previous ruler of the Vale—Jacen, and Karina. Annika would have been killed if she hadn't acted quickly to save herself."

"He only knows all of this because he was screwing Karina," Camelia said snidely, zeroed in on Noah. "Karina *is* the one who told you this. Right?"

The reminder of Noah's previous relationship with the beautiful vampire princess Karina stung.

But I refused to let Camelia get to me.

"If you're trying to shock me, it's not going to work," I said. "Noah's told me all about Karina. He introduced us at the Haven. I met Karina's soul mate Peter there, too. They looked incredibly happy together. Just like I am with Noah." I took Noah's hand and gave him a smile, purposefully rubbing our happiness in Camelia's face.

I should have felt bad, given that the father of Camelia's unborn child was dead and all. But I didn't. Camelia was being a total bitch, and from what Noah had just said, she'd betrayed Annika back in the Vale.

Despite the fact that Camelia was helping us now, she was clearly *not* a nice person. She was only doing all of this for me so she wouldn't get kicked off Avalon.

But still… one part of what Noah had said wouldn't stop nagging at me.

"How did you get the antidote to Annika's transformation potion?" I asked Camelia. "Were you working with Geneva?"

Geneva was the witch who had been helping Annika back then, and who had created the potion that erased and replaced my memories. I was finally accepting that I might never get those memories back. But if Camelia knew where any of Geneva's antidotes were, I wanted to know about it. Maybe I'd be able to get my memories back, after all.

"I wasn't working with Geneva." Camelia smiled smugly. "And I didn't have an antidote pill."

"That's not possible," I said. "Spells and potions can only be reversed with an antidote pill created by the same witch that cast the spell or brewed the potion."

At least, that's what everyone had been telling me for the past few months.

"Thanks for the lesson in witchcraft." Camelia rolled her eyes. "I'm one of the most powerful witches in the world. I *clearly* needed it."

"There's only one thing that could reverse a spell without an antidote pill," Darra chimed in, ignoring Camelia's sarcasm. "Fae magic." My mentor studied Camelia, like she was searching for an answer she wasn't sure she'd get. "But the fae don't give anything away without receiving a twisted form of payment in return. So what did you trade for such powerful magic, Camelia?"

Camelia lowered her hand to her belly and looked out toward the horizon, not saying a word. She didn't look like she was going to budge.

That was fine by me. I didn't want to chitchat with her, anyway. None of us did.

So if it was silence she wanted for the rest of the journey to the satellite island, then that was exactly what she was going to get.

16

RAVEN

THERE WAS no need to worry about manning the boat, thanks to the mages' magic keeping us on course. So we used the time on the sailboat to rest, since we'd need to be at full energy once we landed on the island. That was the first rule Noah had taught me about hunting, after all.

Whenever there's a chance to get some sleep, take it.

The three of them were sleeping in shifts, allowing me to sleep as much as I needed. It was one of the perks of being the one who would be doing the actual hunting. It was also probably because since I still hadn't ignited my Nephilim powers, I remained the weakest of the four of us.

I felt like I'd just fallen asleep, when suddenly Noah

was gently shaking me awake. I glanced at my watch. Three hours had passed.

"Are we there?" I rolled over, rubbing the sleep out of my eyes. I'd been having a hard time sleeping recently, but the rocking boat had practically lulled me unconscious.

"Almost," he said, gazing ahead of us. "Look."

I sat up and looked ahead. Sure enough, the satellite island had come into view.

It was one giant, lush mountain coming out of the sea. While stunning, it was much smaller than Avalon. It must have only been a few miles around the entire thing. There was a beach around the outside, which was nice. But right behind the beach was a dense jungle. The trees were thick right up until the top of the mountain, where there was a big crater that looked like it belonged on the top of a volcano.

"Why does the island look like a volcano?" I asked.

"Because it *is* a volcano." Camelia smirked and stared at it in awe.

"It's dormant," I said. "Right?"

"Complete your task quickly and you won't need to find out."

Of course. Darra had prepared me about how the final Trial would work. The faster I hunted and killed the supernatural placed on the island, the fewer snares would be thrown my way. The longer I took, the more punishments I'd encounter. The Trial was designed that way to incentivize me to hurry up and complete my task.

Soon, the sailboat landed on the beach. We all hopped off and pulled it onto shore. But we couldn't leave it there, sitting in plain sight for anyone to take.

"We need to hide the sailboat," I said, since I'd instantly lose the Trial if Dr. Foster found it and escaped. Plus, we needed it to return to Avalon. Yes, the witches could teleport us back in case of an emergency, but returning by sailboat was a part of the ceremony. "Noah and Darra, can you drag it into the jungle? We can cover it with leaves to camouflage it. Camelia, we'll hide the boat's tracks in the sand."

While the others weren't allowed to help me actually hunt and kill Dr. Foster, they were allowed to help me with tasks like this. And despite how much I didn't like Camelia, I couldn't ask a pregnant person to lug a sailboat across the beach and into the jungle.

Luckily, Noah and Darra were more than up for the task. They didn't even have to drag the sailboat. They simply picked it up and carried it into the jungle. It was situated and hidden amongst the trees in no time.

I inspected their work. It was flawless. No one would

know the sailboat was there if they didn't know to look for it.

"Come on," I said loudly once they were finished. "Let's walk around the island and get our bearings."

They followed me away from the hidden boat. They *had* to follow me, since interfering with my decisions was against the rules of the Trial.

Camelia rolled her eyes as we walked away. She obviously thought I was being stupid.

I smiled inwardly at the knowledge that I was about to one up her.

Once we reached a place where we could still see the location where we'd stashed the boat, but wouldn't be overheard from there if we whispered, I ducked behind a nearby rock. I motioned for the others to do the same, and they did. We all had our cloaking rings on, which masked our scents. So from this spot, we'd be hidden.

"We can keep a lookout from here," I whispered. "Make sure Dr. Foster wasn't nearby and doesn't try taking the boat."

"Smart." Noah nodded in approval.

Darra also looked pleased. Camelia said nothing.

I didn't think Camelia wanted me to fail, since she needed the Nephilim army just as much as every other supernatural in the world. But she definitely didn't want this to be easy for me.

"And if he does try taking the boat?" she asked.

"Then it's the perfect opportunity for me to corner him and ignite my powers."

I almost said it was my perfect opportunity to kill him, but I couldn't. Because I'd be taking a life I didn't think deserved should be taken.

I didn't want to face that fact until I had to.

Hopefully Dr. Foster would do something heinous before that point. Something that would remove my doubts and prove that killing him was the right move.

We waited quietly behind the rock for about an hour. If Dr. Foster was going to take the boat, he would have already made his move by the time the hour was up. It seemed like we were in the clear.

I stood up and stretched. It had been pretty uncomfortable staying in the same spot for so long without moving. The others did the same.

"*Now* we'll walk around the island," I said. "We'll look for any signs of Dr. Foster and try to track him."

Well, *I'd* look for any signs of him. The others weren't allowed to help me. Their supernatural senses of smell would have made it too easy for me.

The rules were frustrating, but they were there so I could prove I deserved to be a Nephilim. And as much as I wished I could break the rules, I wanted respect from the supernatural community. Which meant I had to do this their way.

We started along the beach, walking slightly in the ocean to hide our tracks. The sun shined directly above us, and despite our feet being in the water, it was hot.

I'd grown unused to dealing with extreme temperatures, because Avalon always had perfect weather. Now, I was wiping sweat from my brow, and feeling dehydrated before I should have. I imagined my cheeks were flushed red from the heat.

We were going to have to find fresh water, and eventually, food. Especially for Camelia. Walking in this heat while pregnant couldn't be easy for her. A glance at the others showed me they were okay so far—probably because they were supernaturals and didn't tire out as quickly as I did. But they weren't invincible. And surviving was an important part of the hunt. I had to keep myself strong so I'd be ready for the eventual fight.

But I didn't want to pause on searching for Dr. Foster yet. The more time he had on the island by himself, the harder he was going to be to find. I had to push through for as long as I could before taking a break to locate fresh water.

We continued around the island for another forty-five minutes, when finally I spotted footprints on the beach. They went from the ocean into the jungle.

"Look." I pointed to the footprints going into the dense foliage. "I think we've found the start of our trail."

"Good job." Noah nodded and motioned toward the forest. "Lead the way."

Noah was a leader—I could tell it was taking effort for him not to be the first one to follow the trail. But he wanted me to succeed in the final Trial as much as I did. He wouldn't risk that by breaking the rules.

I led the way into the jungle, and using the techniques Darra taught me during our classroom sessions, I started tracking Dr. Foster's trail.

Tracking in an unknown environment was hard. The best trackers knew the environment inside and out. Since this was the first time I'd seen this island, I had a massive disadvantage here.

But I scanned the area like a canvas, looking out for any clues of his whereabouts, like I was taught. Heel marks first, since the heel was the part of the body that bore the most weight. Look out for any broken branches or other disturbances in the natural environment. I could do this.

And I *did* do it... until the trail grew cold two hours later.

I climbed a tall tree and looked around the jungle, frustrated at Dr. Foster for finally realizing he needed to cover his trail. Maybe he'd even purposefully left a trail taking us in one direction, and then bolted the other way, covering his tracks. The possibilities were endless.

All I knew was that right now, the trail was cold and we needed food and water to continue on. I'd been hoping we'd stumble across fresh water while following Dr. Foster's trail, since he'd eventually need water, too. But that hadn't happened.

Luckily, shifters had the unique ability to smell water. And while Noah couldn't use his supernatural abilities to help me track Dr. Foster, he *could* use them to help me stay alive.

"Noah," I said, turning to him. His wet shirt was sticking to his chest in all the right places. I wanted to run my hands all over his slick, chiseled body. But I forced my lustful thoughts away—especially since Darra and Camelia were looking on. "Can you take us to fresh water?"

I hadn't wanted to ask earlier, because I hadn't wanted to get off track from Dr. Foster's trail. But since we'd already lost the trail, we might as well take the break we needed.

"Of course I can." Noah took a deep breath and turned to face the opposite direction. "This way," he said, motioning for us to follow him.

An hour later, we were sitting around a freshwater pool with a beautiful waterfall cascading down into it.

Behind the waterfall was a cave that could make excellent shelter if we needed it. And since this island was a satellite of Avalon, the water wasn't regular water—it was Holy Water.

Once we'd drank as much Holy Water as possible and filled the empty water bladders we'd brought with us, I scanned the area for mana. Where there was Holy Water, there should be mana. Right?

But there was none in sight.

My stomach rumbled. Yes, the Holy Water quenched my thirst, but the hunger was starting to make me feel lightheaded and weak. I needed food if I wanted to perform on my A-game.

Unfortunately, all I'd seen in the jungle so far in terms of wildlife were bugs, tarantulas, and the occasional frog. There were also snakes, but their bright neon colors made them look poisonous.

Best to stay away from the snakes.

"So." I looked around at the others, already feeling disgusted about what I was about to say. "Who here knows how to cook a tarantula?"

17

RAVEN

STRANGELY ENOUGH, Darra knew how to cook tarantulas. She'd learned during a trip to Cambodia she'd taken in the 1990s. Apparently tarantula was a delicacy of that region. As were frogs.

The supernaturals set out to catch the creatures, since they were faster than I was. I was in charge of starting the fire. Starting a fire was another skill Darra had taught me in our survival classroom sessions. We'd brought pieces of flint with us. So all I needed to do was gather sticks, create a tinder nest, and get the flames going.

Soon after I got the fire going, the others returned with an assortment of tarantulas and frogs. I couldn't believe we were about to *eat* those things.

Desperate times called for desperate measures.

Darra had us skewer the spiders and frogs with sticks and cook them over the open flame. The sun set while we were cooking, and for the first time since we'd arrived at the island, I felt at peace as we chatted around the fire.

About twenty minutes later, the food was cooked and ready to eat.

"With the tarantula, eat the abdomen first," Darra advised. "It's the tastiest part. I'd demonstrate, but since vampires don't need food to survive, I don't want to waste anything we have here on me."

I held the tarantula in front of me, unable to believe we were doing this. Even my rumbling stomach couldn't make the spider look appetizing.

"Scared?" Noah teased, breaking a leg off the tarantula he was holding and popping it in his mouth.

"You should talk." I rolled my eyes. "Starting with a leg instead of the abdomen."

"I like saving the best part for last." He smirked and popped another leg into his mouth.

I held onto the leg of my spider, dangling it in front of myself. Gross. But staring at the tarantula wasn't going to make this easier. It was probably best to just go for it.

So I did as Darra said and took a huge bite of the abdomen, getting it all in one go.

It was weirdly squishy. And hairy. And bland. I wasn't sure what I'd expected the spider to taste like, but it certainly hadn't been that. I made a face as I chewed. The meat left a strange texture in my mouth, and I had to drink water to flush it out.

"It's that bad?" Noah asked.

"Tastes like chicken," I said brightly, smiling and going in for another bite.

It took all of my efforts not to gag. But somehow, I forced down the rest of the spider. The first bite had been the hardest. After that, my body had been so happy to finally be getting food that I continued on, trying not to think too much about the fact that I was eating a *spider*. Because yuck. It was gross no matter how I tried to think about it.

I wished we had our phones on us so we could record this. No one would believe me without video evidence.

We finished off the tarantulas and frogs, not letting any go to waste. Camelia ate more than Noah—I supposed her pregnancy was increasing her appetite. If she was disgusted by the food, she didn't show it.

She was one tough woman. I would have admired her if she'd ever shown a bit of warmth or compassion in that icy heart of hers.

Just as we were finishing the meal, the sky lit up with

lightning, and thunder sounded from down near the ocean. The air felt like it was thickening. It smelled like rain.

I looked up at the sky in dread.

"Sounds like a storm's brewing," I said.

"The first sign that you're losing time," Camelia said.

Thunder rumbled from above again, louder this time. I frowned and held out a hand as a large drop of rain splattered onto it. If this was a sign I was losing time, it meant Camelia and the witches had planned this storm when they'd prepared the island for my Trial.

It was going to be a nasty one.

"There's a cave around the side of the waterfall," I said, glad I'd scouted the area when we'd arrived. Darra's teachings were coming in handy. "We should go there for shelter until the storm passes."

We gathered what was left of the food, refilled out water bladders up to the tops, and hurried toward the cave. On our way there, the sky opened up above, dumping buckets of rain onto us. We were soaked by the time we got inside.

Our Avalon Academy jumpsuits dried once we were in the cave, thanks to the magic the mages had put on them. Our hair wasn't as lucky.

But when I glanced up, I was no longer thinking about my wet hair.

Because the top of the cave was magically lit up like the Northern Lights. The greens, pinks, and purples swirled on the ceiling, creating light in what would have otherwise been darkness. It was so beautiful that it took my breath away.

The storm gathered strength outside the cave, blowing wind and rain inside. I wrapped my arms around myself to try to stop shivering. We could go deeper inside the cave, but we had no idea how bad this storm would get. We needed more protection from the outside. Especially because the wind was gathering strength so quickly. It sounded like a hurricane out there.

"Camelia," I said, looking toward the witch. She was staring pensively out of the cave, and her face brightened as a bolt of lightning struck down close to the entrance.

She didn't jump like the rest of us did.

"Yes?" she asked.

"Is there a spell to keep the wind and rain from entering the cave?"

"A light magic boundary spell will keep anything from entering," she said simply.

"Great," I said. "Please cast one for us. Make it last for the rest of the time we're on this island. Who knows when else we'll need it."

"As you wish." She turned to the cave entrance, rose up her hands, and started mumbling in Latin. Bright yellow light glowed from her palms, expanding all the way to the cave entrance as she cast the spell that would keep us dry and safe.

After about a minute, the light from her palms died down and disappeared. Rain and wind was visible outside, but it was like a shield had been placed at the cave entrance, stopping it from coming in. It was quiet for the first time since the storm had started. Eerily so, given the storm beating down outside like a hurricane.

The spell was in place. And now that the outside elements weren't coming inside, the inside of the cave was warm and comfortable.

"It looks like we'll be in here until the storm passes," I said, disappointed in myself for not finding Dr. Foster before the first marking point of lost time. But it was what it was. All I could do now was move forward. "We should use this time to rest. Then, once it clears up, we'll be ready to resume our hunt."

18

RAVEN

LIKE ON THE SAILBOAT, the supernaturals slept in shifts, allowing me to sleep straight through the night.

This time, Darra was the one to wake me up. She woke Noah, too, since we were sleeping in each other's arms. Camelia was already awake.

"The storm has stopped," she said once we sat up and blinked away the haze of sleep.

I looked out the entrance of the cave. Sure enough, peaceful pinks and yellows shined down outside—the light of the sun rising. The storm must have lasted the entire night. The only sign of the storm was the leaves and other debris spread out on the ground. Other than that, all looked calm.

Suddenly, the trees across from us rustled. It looked like something—or some*one*—was out there.

"Something moved." I reached for Excalibur, which was strapped to my weapons belt, and held it up. Sleeping with the sword had been uncomfortable, but there was no way I was parting with my weapon. "I'm going to investigate. I'll be allowed back inside the cave boundary, right?" I directed the last part toward Camelia.

"The four of us can come and go from the cave as we please," she said. "Anyone else will be blocked from entering. It's the same spell I cast around the Vale when I was the main witch there, although on a much smaller scale."

"Good." I nodded, confident of Camelia's ability, and hurried out of the cave. I didn't want whatever it was I'd seen moving in the jungle to get too far away.

I stayed as quiet as possible as I walked toward the trees. The others followed behind, doing their job to keep me safe. They followed the entire time I tracked the path.

I stopped mid-step when I finally caught sight of what I was tracking.

A wild boar. Brown in color, it must have been at least three feet tall and five feet long. Its butt was toward us, its snout buried in the tree roots it was eating. From the intense way it was chowing down, you'd think it hadn't had a meal in ages.

Maybe it had been waiting to venture out until after the storm, too.

Disappointment slammed into me at the realization that I wasn't any closer to finding Dr. Foster. But as I gazed at the boar, hunger hit me too. Both my own, since tarantulas and frogs hadn't been the most filling meal ever, and Noah's coming through the imprint bond.

From the way Noah was licking his lips and staring hungrily at the boar, I guessed they were a big food source for wolves. Which made sense, given his love for bacon.

Before any of the supernaturals could act, I ran at the boar, raised my sword, and sliced the animal straight through the neck. The sword lit on fire as I moved it, cooking the boar's exposed flesh in the process.

Both the body and head of the boar collapsed to the ground. I'd killed it so quickly that it wouldn't have known what was happening. The death itself took only a second, and would have been as close to painless as possible.

I was glad of it, since it was an innocent creature. I hadn't wanted it to suffer. I'd always been a meat eater, but I'd never hunted for my food before. It was harder to make the kill myself as opposed to buying a packet of meat from the grocery store. But we needed a more substantial meal, since spiders and frogs weren't going to cut it, and the boar had basically landed at our feet.

As much as I tried to rationalize it, I still felt bad. But it was already done, and we'd needed the sustenance. It was natural for humans to hunt animals for food. So there was no point in beating myself up about it.

I lowered the sword, the fire disappearing from the blade, and placed it back in my weapons belt. When I turned around to face the others, they were all staring at me with mixes of shock, awe, and hunger.

"So... who wants to help me bring our breakfast inside?" I asked.

I didn't need to say anything more before Noah and Darra hurried over to the boar, picked it up, and carried it into the cave.

19

RAVEN

THE BOAR MEAT WAS DELICIOUS. The animal was so big that we barely made a dent in it, but Camelia was able to cast a spell on the leftovers to keep them fresh for the rest of the time we'd be on the island. We were keeping it in the cave, since the cave was quickly becoming our home base.

Once we were finished eating, we headed back out to resume tracking Dr. Foster. As I suspected, the storm had wiped out most of the tracks we'd been following yesterday. We were basically back to square one. I just hoped he hadn't gone much farther from where I'd lost his trail before.

For hours, I walked aimlessly through the jungle, searching for any hints about where he might be. I was careful to remember where I'd searched, so I wouldn't retrace my steps. The last thing I needed was to waste time. I didn't know what the next punishment would be for taking too long, but after that awful storm, I didn't want to find out.

Noah eventually led us to another, smaller freshwater pond. While filling up our water bladders, I spotted something in the ground that made my heart jump in excitement.

Footprints identical to the ones we'd been tracking yesterday.

Dr. Foster must have been here recently to get water.

I pointed out the footprints to the others, motioning for them to be quiet. If Dr. Foster was within hearing distance, he knew we were here, anyway. But I didn't want him to know we'd caught sight of his trail.

All thought of a water break was forgotten, and we were back into hunting mode. I led the way, the others following behind.

Finally, we came across Dr. Foster.

The old man was huddled at the trunk of a giant tree. The tree branches extended far out and low, curved downward in a way that made me think this was where he'd found shelter from the storm. His clothes were drenched and he was shaking, staring at us with eyes wide in fear.

I reached for my sword, but didn't pull it out of my

weapons belt. Because looking at the pathetic, weak man before me, I couldn't bring myself to kill him in cold blood.

"Please, don't." His voice was small, shaking as he spoke. "I know you have no reason to spare me after what I put you through in the bunker. But you have to understand—I had no choice. My circle is working with the demons. If I didn't cooperate, I would have been thrown out and excommunicated. Penniless, with nowhere to go."

"You did have a choice," I said. "The Haven offers sanctuary to all supernaturals in need. If you'd been honest with them, they would have taken you in."

"The Haven hates Foster witches as much as any other kingdom," he said. "They would have sent me away. Or they would have kept me there and forced me to turn on my family."

"The price to pay for safety," I said, although I knew in my heart that it wasn't so easy.

"As much as I don't agree with everything my family does, I still love them," he said. "They're all I have in this world. I couldn't take that risk."

I studied him, wanting to see the monster everyone claimed he was. But all I saw was a weak, pathetic man who'd been born into the wrong family and was now paying the price.

I believed what I'd said that he should have tried harder to break free, and not allowed his family to walk over him so much. He should have made his own life for himself instead of following the commands of the Foster circle. But did he deserve to die?

I didn't think so.

"If you're going to kill me, do it already," he begged. "I won't fight you. But please make it quick." He curled into himself, staring up at me in fear as he waited for me to take his life.

Now that I'd found him, he was making this easy for me. Just like Camelia and the others at Avalon expected he would.

But was the easiest path the right path?

"I'm not going to kill you," I decided, moving my hand away from the handle of my sword.

"What?" Camelia and Dr. Foster said at the same time. Both of them looked at me like I'd lost my mind.

"I won't kill him," I repeated, staring at Camelia as I spoke. "He's done terrible things, but he's not evil. I couldn't live with myself if I killed him like this."

"Killing him is what you've been sent here to do," Darra said, her voice firm and strong.

I hadn't expected Darra to take Camelia's side. But then again, what *had* I expected? My trainer had come here knowing what I was going to do. She supported it fully.

I looked to Noah, hoping for him to back me up.

"I'll support you no matter what," he said. "But Raven… think for a second. This is your final Trial. Your mom's life and Sage's life count on you completing the Angel Trials and becoming a full Nephilim. Do you really want to put them in danger because of this man you don't know? A man who's been sentenced to death by one of the most powerful vampire kingdoms in the world?"

He was trying to be nice about it, but I could tell he thought I was making the wrong decision, too.

None of it changed my mind. And now I felt as confused as ever.

"I can't keep discussing this in front of him," I said, motioning to Dr. Foster. It felt wrong to talk about his life so casually when he was listening. We needed to go somewhere else to have this conversation.

But I also didn't want to leave any of the others alone with Dr. Foster. Firstly, because I had no idea what they'd do to him. Secondly, because I wanted them all there for the discussion we needed to have.

"Camelia, can you cast a spell around Dr. Foster to make sure he stays under this tree?" I asked.

"I can." She raised her hands and cast a similar spell

around the tree as she had in the cave. But this time, she removed a vial of blood from her weapons belt and used a bit of it in the process.

I knew what that meant—this spell was dark magic. She'd used light magic earlier to keep things *out* of our cave, but had to use dark magic to keep Dr. Foster prisoner.

"Done," she said, once the glow around the tree dimmed down to nothing. "It's a single prison spell for one person. He won't be able to leave for twenty-four hours. But if anyone else—specifically, any of us—go into the space, we'll be able to come and go as we please. And don't try to scream for us," she warned Dr. Foster. "There's a sound spell blocking us from hearing you. Nothing you try to say can or will impact us."

"Thanks." I nodded to her, remaining as calm and courteous as ever. "Let's go back to the pond to discuss the plan from here." The pond had been close by, but far enough away that Dr. Foster wouldn't be able to over-hear our conversation.

I marched back to the pond, not looking behind me as the others followed my lead. I couldn't bring myself to look at any of them—not even Noah. I thought they'd be more supportive of me back there. Well, I at least thought Noah would be. He hadn't exactly been *unsup-*

portive, but still, I'd been hoping for more than what he'd given me.

He knew me well enough to stay back and give me time to think as we walked.

I finally turned back to them once we reached the pond.

Darra crossed her arms, fierce and angry. "What were you thinking?" she asked. "We've been training for this for months. You had a perfect shot at him. If you'd taken it, you'd be a Nephilim right now."

"I've been training to kill *demons* for months," I said. "You know—the red-eyed monsters trying to steal Earth from the humans and supernaturals who live there. I haven't been training to kill weak male witches dragged into doing their evil family's bidding because of an unfortunate circumstance of birth."

Camelia narrowed her beady eyes at me and swatted a fly away from her face. "Dr. Foster is the one we selected for you to kill for this Trial," she said. "So he's exactly who you've been training to kill."

"No." I leveled my gaze with hers. I'd given in the first time we'd had this conversation, but now that I'd seen Dr. Foster again—and seen how weak and pathetic he was—I wasn't going to give in again. "I'll never be able to live with myself if I murder him in cold blood.

Because that's what it would be. Murder. And I'm better than that."

Noah walked over to stand beside me. Now it was the two of us facing Camelia and Darra. Noah had never been a man of many words, but his standing behind me meant only one thing—he was taking my side. He also trusted me to win this argument on my own.

I gave him a single nod, grateful for his support.

An insect tried flying into my eye, and I swatted it away. It landed on my neck and stung me, and I swatted it again. Gross.

The sooner we were off this island, the better.

"Now that you've survived drinking from the Holy Grail, you think mighty highly of yourself, don't you?" Camelia asked with an amused chuckle.

"As a matter of fact, yes." I stood strong, not letting her get to me. "I'm the only chance you have right now at creating a full Nephilim. So it's time you do things my way."

Darra smirked and lowered her arms. It appeared my trainer was coming around to my side. Then she swatted at a group of flies buzzing around her.

Noah caught a fly between his fingers and smushed it.

There hadn't been this many insects around before. I

looked around in confusion. Where were they all coming from?

"What exactly is 'your way?'" Camelia asked.

"I know you wanted me to kill Dr. Foster because he's so weak that I'd definitely beat him in a fight," I said. "But I've been training to kill demons for months. So I want you to teleport off this island and find a demon for me to slay instead. A lower level one." The last bit should have been obvious, since I could only kill greater demons *after* coming into my Nephilim powers. But there was no harm in being as clear as possible. "I want to know that the creature I'm killing deserves it."

And as I'd learned in my lessons, all demons deserved it. They were psychopaths without a conscience. They were plagues upon the Earth, and they needed to be killed. All of them.

"The Vale is holding a few lower level demons in their prison for experiments," Camelia said. "I suppose I can go to King Alexander and see if he's willing to relinquish one for your Trial."

"Really?" My mouth dropped open, but I closed it before a fly could get inside. "That easily?"

"We need you to come into your Nephilim powers," she said. "If you refuse to kill Dr. Foster, you're not giving me much of a choice but to find another way for you to ignite those powers, are you?"

"Nope." I beamed. There was nothing quite like the rush of winning an argument.

"But first, we have another problem," she said.

"What's that?"

She pointed behind me, and I turned around to see what she meant.

A wall of insects was flying toward us, their buzzing getting louder by the second. I must have been so consumed by our conversation that I hadn't been listening closely enough.

"You're losing time," she said. "The second plague is here."

20

RAVEN

THE INSECTS WERE FLYING FASTER than I could run. So I looked around, searching for shelter. But unlike at the lake, there was no cave here for us to hide in. And our cave was hours away by foot.

It looked like we'd be taking on the insects directly.

I reached for Excalibur and held it up in front of me, fire burning around the blade.

"You're going to attack insects with your sword?" Noah cocked his head in amusement.

"Maybe they'll be scared of the blade and will keep their distance," I said. "You plan on helping or not?"

He removed his dagger from his weapons belt, and we started swinging our blades at the wall of buzzing insects. I spotted Darra and Camelia out of the corner of my eyes doing the same.

The blades helped, but not much. The flies were still landing on me and stinging.

Each sting was like a pinprick of burning. It hurt worse and worse each time, and was spreading through my body. I wanted to curl up into a ball, cover my ears with my hands, and wish the stupid insects away.

But that wouldn't solve any problems. Instead, I looked around the area, trying to see if there was anywhere the insects weren't going. My first thought was that maybe we could climb a tall tree and get out of their range. But the wall of them seemed to go up forever.

Deciding that was hopeless, I looked down to the ground. The wall of them went all the way to the dirt, too. So much for that.

I kept swinging my blade, but there were too many of them to take down with weapons. And the bites stung so badly. I wanted to jump into the pond of Holy Water to cool down.

With that thought, I looked toward the pond and gasped. Because the water—and up to a foot above it— was clear of insects.

They were avoiding the Holy Water.

"Guys!" I screamed, loudly enough to be heard over the incessant buzzing. "Follow me!"

I secured my sword on my weapons belt, ran toward the pond, and dove in.

My skin instantly cooled. Surrounded by water, the buzzing went away, everything around me going bless-edly quiet. I heard three splashes nearby—the others diving in.

When I came up for air, I kept my head as close to the surface as possible. The others did the same. Since the flies weren't getting close to the water, it allowed us enough space to breathe. Once we realized the pond was a safe zone, we moved closer to the edge, where our feet could touch the bottom.

Noah brought an arm down to hit the surface of the water, splashing it up into the flies.

The water disintegrated the flies on contact.

"Nice." I also splashed the flies, smiling when they disintegrated as well.

The Holy Water destroyed them. I splashed again, watching the flies I hit disappear. Amazing.

Camelia and Darra splashed them too. There were way too many flies for us to kill them all, but after the way the insects had attacked us, it felt good to get back at them.

Before I knew it, we'd all gotten in a water fight, and were squealing and laughing as we splashed each other and the flies. Even Camelia was partaking in the fun.

Eventually, we tired and stopped the splashing. I did a back float, staring up at the masses of insects above me. "Will Dr. Foster be okay?" I asked. "He's trapped in that boundary and can't run away…"

"He'll be fine," Camelia said. "The plagues are designed to avoid him. Killing him was supposed to be your job."

I rolled my eyes. We were back to that now, were we?

But she'd already agreed to my terms, so I wasn't going to let her words bother me.

"How long until the flies go away?" I asked instead.

"I can't tell you that," Camelia said. Of course she couldn't—she'd created the spells as a punishment for me. It was against the rules for her to give away their secrets. "But we'll be safe waiting here until they pass."

"Great," I said. "Since we're safe, how about you teleport to the Vale right now and talk to King Alexander about bringing a lower level demon here so I can kill it and ignite my powers?"

I was sick of being a weak human. The sooner I could ignite my Nephilim powers, the better.

And I was thrilled I'd get to do it *my* way. Yes, Dr. Foster was still sentenced to death—a situation that didn't sit well with me—but at least it didn't have to be by my hand.

"The sooner you ignite your powers, the better,"

Camelia said. "I'll see you soon. And when I'm back with that demon, you better not let me down."

I waited for her to teleport away.

But she remained in the pond, staring straight ahead. She stood there a few seconds more, her brows creasing in frustration.

My stomach sank in dread. "What's wrong?" I asked.

"I can't teleport." Her eyes darted around, trapped. "It feels like there's a boundary spell around the entire island. Like the one I cast around Dr. Foster, but bigger."

"Are you sure?" Noah asked. "Or could you be having issues with your powers because of your pregnancy?"

"I already told you that the pregnancy strengthens my powers—it doesn't weaken them." She narrowed her eyes at him, like she thought he was an imbecile for asking.

It had been my first thought too, but I said nothing. Best to explore other options before returning to that one.

"Can you still teleport around the island?" Darra asked.

"Good question." Camelia refocused, and flashed out.

She reappeared in the exact same place a few seconds later.

"Where'd you go?" I asked.

"Back to the cave," she said. "So yes, I can still teleport around the island. I just can't leave or send any fire messages through the boundary around it. None of us can."

"Who would have cast a spell like that around the island?" I asked. "Who else but us can even *get* to this island?" Only the citizens of Avalon knew the location of this satellite island. And no one on Avalon wished me harm. If they did, they wouldn't have made it past King Arthur's simulation.

"A dark magic spell big enough to contain us on an entire island could only be cast by an extremely strong dark witch," Camelia said, her voice taking on a chilling tone. "Dark magic that strong hasn't been seen since the time of the Foster circle."

A whirlwind of thoughts raced through my mind. I didn't know where to start. It didn't help that the flies were still buzzing like crazy above our heads, making it hard to think.

This plague needed to end already.

"I don't understand." I blinked, trying to process what was going on. "Dr. Foster has no magic. He couldn't have cast the spell."

"No," Camelia confirmed. "He couldn't have. Especially not through the boundary I cast around him."

"So did someone from his circle come to rescue him?" I asked. "How did they even find this island? And if they did come to rescue him, why cast a spell to keep us locked in here? Why not just take him and leave? Because they have to stay close for the spell to keep working... right?"

At least, that was what I thought I remembered from my academy classes about dark magic boundary spells.

"Whoa." Camelia held her hands up for me to slow down. But she looked as troubled as I felt, which didn't sit well with me. "One question at a time."

"They're good questions," Darra said. "They all deserve addressing."

"Yes, a spell this large and strong can only be maintained as long as the witch who cast it remains in close proximity," Camelia said, answering my last question first.

"But the only reason to stay and lock us in here would be to fight us," I said.

Noah nodded. Apparently he'd already drawn the same conclusion. We looked at each other, and I knew he was thinking the same thing as me.

My final Trial was about to get a *lot* more interesting.

"I know you said you won't fight Dr. Foster," Darra said. "But this other dark witch here... would you consider fighting her?"

"I'd more than consider it." I felt for Excalibur's handle in the water, and the weapon buzzed with energy in my grip. The female Foster witches had been actively using their magic to ally with Azazel. They weren't any better than the demons themselves. "I'm ready for it."

21

RAVEN

UNFORTUNATELY, I couldn't hunt down the female Foster witch just yet. We had to wait another hour for the flies to clear.

Once they were gone, we hurried back to the tree where we'd left Dr. Foster.

When we arrived back at the tree, I recoiled in disgust.

Dr. Foster was sprawled out on the ground. His vacant eyes stared out at us, and blood puddled beneath him. Numerous claw marks had torn through his clothes and into his skin. It looked like a wild animal had mutilated him. A bear, or a tiger, or a lion or something.

I didn't need to check for a pulse to know he was dead.

If the Foster witch who'd cast the boundary spell around the island had come to rescue him, she'd done a terrible job of it. Something else was going on here.

"Crap." I backed away from the body and looked at the others. "What do we do now?"

"I still can't teleport off the island," Camelia said. "Whoever did this to him must still be here."

My eyes met Noah's, and neither of us had to speak to know what the other was thinking. Because whoever had done this to Dr. Foster had to be after us next.

"Can you guys smell a dark witch anywhere?" I asked.

Sure, they weren't supposed to help me during my final Trial. But now that the Trial had been breached, surely the rules could be thrown out the window.

No one had a chance to answer before a huge figure dropped down from the top of the tree. He crouched down in front of us, his red eyes gleaming as he grinned maliciously.

Azazel.

I reached for my sword at the same time as Noah and Darra reached for theirs.

But I didn't have a chance to pull the sword out of my weapons belt before Camelia flashed to my side, grabbed my arm, and teleported us back to the cave.

When I raised my sword above my head, she'd

already flashed back out. I was standing in the cave alone. Well, it was just me and what was left of the boar. But he didn't count.

A few seconds later, Camelia returned with Darra. Then she flashed out again, returning with Noah a few seconds after that.

Once I confirmed they were all unharmed, I turned to Camelia, furious. "What was that for?" I fumed, my sword still raised and flaming in front of me. The shadows of the flames danced across the cave walls. "I have Excalibur. I could have killed Azazel."

"No, you couldn't have." Camelia was as levelheaded as ever. "Excalibur is a strong sword—the most magical in the world. But not even Excalibur can slay a greater demon if it's not wielded by a Nephilim. By bringing you back here, I saved you. I saved *all* of you." She looked to Noah and Darra, punctuating her point.

"How do you know Excalibur can't slay Azazel on its own?" I asked. "You didn't give me a chance to *try*."

"Witches make it our business to study the history of the supernatural world." She held her chin up high like the snob she was. "Once you pulled Excalibur from the stone, I brushed up on its history. It can kill lower demons, like any other holy weapon. But only Nephilim have enough magic to slay a greater demon, Excalibur or no. If you'd tried fighting Azazel, you would have wasted valuable energy and likely gotten yourself killed. I just saved your life. A little gratitude would be nice right now."

"Great." I shoved the sword back into my weapons belt, trying to think of a new plan. "I guess we have to find that dark witch who's here, don't we?" I asked, mustering more confidence into my tone than I was feeling right now. "So I can kill her, become a Nephilim, and take care of Azazel once and for all."

Now that Dr. Foster was dead, the other Foster witch on this island seemed my best chance of becoming a Nephilim. I just had to find her and kill her *without* Azazel finding and killing me first.

This was going to be tough.

It was a good thing I had Noah, Darra, and Camelia on my side to help.

Suddenly, something big slammed against the invisible boundary wall that covered the entry to the cave.

Azazel.

How had he found us so quickly?

He kept throwing himself at the wall, trying to force his way in. Luckily, the boundary was strong enough to keep him out. But that didn't stop him from continuing to try.

Each time he collided with the invisible barrier, my heart beat faster, and dread built in my stomach. Before, at least I stood a chance of finding the Foster witch before Azazel found us.

Now we were trapped on this island, cornered by a greater demon none of us could kill. How were we all supposed to get out of this alive?

I looked around at the others, hoping one of them had a brilliant idea. But they all looked as concerned as I felt.

This wasn't good.

I glanced back at Azazel. He'd stopped throwing himself at the wall. Now his lips were moving, although we couldn't hear a word thanks to the soundproof boundary Camelia had cast to keep out the sounds of the storm.

"He's trying to talk to us," I said. "Can you let us hear what he's saying without weakening the barrier?"

"I can." Camelia nodded and raised her arms to perform the spell. Her bright yellow magic shot out toward the cave entrance, lighting the boundary up so it glowed. After a few seconds, the yellow glow dimmed out and disappeared.

Azazel tried strolling into the cave, but he walked straight into the invisible wall. "Damn it," he said, rubbing his nose. "I thought you were being nice and letting me in."

"Why would we do that?" I walked straight up to the boundary and crossed my arms, not wanting to look intimidated.

"Because of the deal I offered you." He smirked.

That must have been what he was rambling on about when we couldn't hear him. "I'd never take a deal from you," I said. "Save your energy."

"Are you so sure about that?" He raised an eyebrow. "Because unless you plan on killing one of your friends in there with you—which I know you won't do, since your heart is so soft you couldn't even bring yourself to hurt dear old Dr. Foster—you're at my mercy. It might benefit you to hear me out."

"You're talking like my friends here are the only other supernaturals on this island." I somehow managed to sound a lot more confident than I felt. "Like your witch isn't hiding in the shadows somewhere, waiting for us to find her."

"My witch isn't on this island anymore," he said. "She wouldn't leave herself vulnerable like that. She cast the spell and left."

"Impossible." Noah growled. "She needs to stay on the island to maintain the spell."

"Maybe a normal witch would need to stay on the island." Azazel shrugged. "A Foster witch doesn't."

I spun around to look at Camelia. "Is that true?" I asked.

"The Fosters use ancient magic," she said. "It's different from the magic used by any other witch circle. So yes, it's possible."

"Great," I muttered. Just when I thought the situation couldn't get any worse, it did.

My other Trials had gone so smoothly. I supposed it was too much to hope that this one would be the same.

"It is great." Azazel smirked again. "And you know what's even better? The deal I was offering you. Why don't you let me in your humble abode here so we can discuss it?"

"In your dreams," I said. "If you want us to hear your deal so badly, tell us from out there."

I had no intention on taking him up on any deal. But humoring him wouldn't do any harm… and it would also buy us time to figure out what to do from here. Maybe he'd slip up and say something we could use to our advantage. And Darra was being pretty quiet so far —hopefully she was coming up with a plan.

"You're being cautious," he said. "I can respect that."

I said nothing, waiting for him to continue.

"I want all of you to come over to my side," he said.

"Come live with me and the others in the Montgomery compound, where you'll be safe. Do that, and all of your past transgressions will be forgotten. Easy."

"Seriously?" I scoffed. "You really expect us to say yes to that?"

He was either playing with us, or he was delusional. I suspected the former.

"I do," he said. "You see, Raven, your mom is already staying with me. Now that she's a vampire, she's a powerful prophetess. How else do you think I knew to find you in that alley in Chicago, and now here on this island? She told me where you were. She wants me to bring you home to her. She wants you to join our side." He smirked, apparently thinking he was getting somewhere. "Isn't that what you want? To be with your mom again? Because she wants to be with you."

I narrowed my eyes at him, believing none of it. "My mom would never betray me like that," I said.

"She would, and she did," he said. "Come with me. I'll have you turned into a vampire too, and you can be reunited with your mom. We'll be one big happy family. Noah, too." He turned to Noah, his eyes glinting with excitement. "I know all about the First Prophet of the Vale. You were the driving force that helped open the Hell Gate and free us from that rotting place below, giving us a chance at a new life on Earth. You're a legend amongst our kind. Of course you'll be welcomed back. We'll do a blood binding ceremony to make it official and everything."

I shivered at the mention of the blood binding ceremony. That was what Azazel had used on Sage and the other Montgomery shifters. The spell that bound their souls to him and took away their free will.

I'd never let that happen to Noah.

"Keep dreaming, Azazel," Noah said, apparently not fazed in the slightest. His hand was wrapped around his dagger, and his entire body was tense, like it was taking all his self-control not to run up to Azazel and run the weapon straight through his heart.

I stepped away from Azazel, moving to Noah's side. I trusted Noah to control himself and not make any sudden moves against the greater demon. But I felt better being closer to him.

"Darra and Camelia here will make extraordinary additions to my growing family, too," Azazel said, ignoring Noah's comment. "Darra is one of the strongest fighters from the Ward Kingdom—a vampire kingdom that only drinks the blood of children, if I'm not mistaken?" He looked to me after saying that last part, as if he expected me to be surprised.

Darra remained as calm as ever. "You've been doing your research," she said. "Good job."

"Thank you." He grinned. "I have."

If he was trying to use Darra's past to shock me, it wasn't going to work. I already knew all about the Ward Kingdom, where Darra had lived before coming to Avalon. Yes, they survived on the blood of children, which was admittedly disturbing. But they kept the children alive. It was more than the Tower Kingdom did with their victims, who were all murdered outright.

But everyone had a fresh start once they came through King Arthur's simulation and entered Avalon. Even the vampires from the Tower and Carpathian Kingdoms—the most brutal of the six vampire kingdoms.

"On Avalon, we judge each other on who we are on the island," I said, holding my gaze with Azazel's. "Not on who we were before it."

"Because of that rowboat ride through the fog you go on to get there," he said. "Correct? The fog brings you to some other world, where you're judged on your inner character and either given entrance to Avalon or sent away."

"How do you know that?" I asked.

"I have my ways." He smirked. "Your mother isn't the only one who's found herself in my care. How do you think I was able to locate this satellite island? Only a

131

gifted vampire with an excellent sense of direction would be able to find it…"

"Kara," I said, my heart dropping as I put it together.

From his amused expression, I'd guessed correctly.

"How did you get her?"

"Details for another time." He waved off my question. "Because Camelia here was a vicious little witch back when she lived at the Vale." He looked to her, smiling. "You didn't have to go through the simulation, did you?" he asked. "You wouldn't have made it through if you had."

"Why do you ask?" she said.

"I'm just curious," he said. "So tell me. Am I right?"

"You are." She stepped forward, looking as smug as ever. "I had a deal with the Earth Angel. She brought me straight to Avalon, and I've been safe there since."

"Camelia," I said, warning in my tone. I hadn't known she hadn't gone through the simulation. But why was she telling Azazel this? He was clearly baiting her. She was too smart to give into his mind games so easily.

She ignored me. "Avalon hasn't been what I expected," she continued. "It's boring, and the Earth Angel's army is… underwhelming, to say the least." She glanced at me, like I was the underwhelming one for not killing Dr. Foster when I had the chance.

I *knew* she looked down on me for it. But how was this any of Azazel's business?

Camelia had always been cold and icy. Now, she sounded soulless.

I opened my mouth to say something—anything—to stop this. But before I could, she refocused on Azazel and said the last thing I expected.

"If you have a deal that will tempt me to join your side, I'm all ears. So please, tell me more."

22

RAVEN

I LOOKED at Camelia in shock. She couldn't mean it.

But from the intense, interested way she studied Azazel, she appeared to seriously be considering his proposition.

I hoped this was all some grand plan of hers.

Then again, I'd felt like there was something off about her since meeting her. And she'd just admitted to not having to go through the simulation to get to Avalon.

I wanted to trust that she wouldn't betray us. But after learning on the way here about the way she'd betrayed the Earth Angel back at the Vale... I couldn't be sure.

Maybe she'd just been buying herself time back at

Avalon until a better offer came along. And now, that offer was here.

"Join my side, and you'll be protected in the upcoming war," Azazel said. "The demons are going to beat the humans and the supernaturals. We're far more powerful—winning is inevitable. Allying with me is the smart move. It's the move that will keep you safe."

Every word he spoke made me feel sick to my stomach. Camelia couldn't be buying this. Could she be?

"An interesting proposal." Camelia took a few steps forward, until she was only a foot away from Azazel. Only the invisible boundary stood between them. The air seemed to crackle with electricity as they held each other's gazes. "But if I go with you, I need to be untraceable to everyone. The other witch circles, the vampires, the fae, the mages, and even the angels. Can your Foster witches do that for me?"

"I had a feeling you'd see things my way." Azazel grinned and eyed her up, checking her out. "Lavinia told me all about you. You're nearly as powerful as the Fosters... and nearly as dark, too. I like it."

"Answer the question," Camelia said, clearly not in the mood to play around.

"Yes," he said simply. "The Foster witches can grant that request. No problem."

"If you're wrong, the deal is off," she said. "Understood?"

"Understood," Azazel said.

"Lovely." Camelia smiled and rested her hands protectively over her protruding stomach. "But it's going to take more to convince the others of reason. I'm going to strengthen the barrier again so I can discuss this with them in private and convince them to see this our way. Can you stay right where you are?"

"If you weren't trapped on this island, I'd worry you were going to turn on me," Azazel said, his voice warm and threatening all at once. It made for a terrifying combination. "But since you're not going anywhere, do as you please. I'll be right here, waiting for you when you're done."

"I expect nothing else." Camelia raised her hands, muttered a spell in Latin, and shot her yellow magic out of her palms and toward the barrier. Like before, the magic glowed as it did its job.

But this time, the barrier didn't remain clear. It became foggy, until we couldn't see through it at all. We couldn't hear through it again, either.

The yellow glow dimmed out, and Camelia turned to face us. Determination gleamed in her eyes.

"You don't seriously think you're going to convince us to join Azazel's side," I said immediately. "Because it's not going to happen." I reached for my sword—I could fight her if it came down to it. I didn't want to, since the last thing I wanted was to hurt her unborn child. But if she made an attempt on any of our lives, I'd have to defend myself.

"Of course not," she said, and I relaxed, but not completely. "But I was the most likely of the four of us to jump on his plan. I had to pretend I was on board with it, so he wouldn't be suspicious when I told him I needed to speak with the three of you privately."

Noah stared straight at her. His expression was unreadable—I only knew he was still suspicious because I felt it through the imprint bond. "You're only on Avalon because the fae are out to get you," he said.

"What makes you think that?" she asked.

"You all but admitted to it on the boat ride here," he said. "You made a deal with the fae in exchange for that potion to reveal Annika's true identity. But you don't want to follow through with that deal. You're on Avalon to hide from them. And for some reason, the Earth Angel is on board. Knowing the Earth Angel, it's for the sake of your child and not for you. Am I onto something here?"

"Yes," Camelia said, shocking me with her honesty. "Avalon is the only place in the world where I can remain hidden from the fae. Azazel's claim that the

Foster witches can hide me from them is wrong. Even if there were a chance he was telling the truth, it wouldn't matter. I'd never risk my safety and the safety of my daughter on the word of a demon. I can't leave the protection of Avalon. Not ever." She placed her hand protectively on her stomach, and I had a gut feeling she was telling the truth.

Camelia was a terrible person. But she'd do anything to protect her child. And making a deal with a greater demon didn't fit into that plan.

"Good," I said. "I was worried you'd switched sides."

"Don't be relieved yet," she said. "Because I know how we can beat Azazel. That's why I needed the four of us to talk in private. But you're not going to like it."

"I'm open to anything," I said.

"I think I know Camelia's plan," Darra said, and all eyes went to her, since she'd been quiet up until now. She had a look on her face that I'd never seen on her before. Acceptance, perhaps? Or resolve. "And she's right. You're not going to like it."

"Why not?" I braced myself, ready for anything.

"Because to beat Azazel, you have to ignite your Nephilim powers," Darra said. "And to do that, you're going to have to kill me."

23

RAVEN

"WHAT?" I backed away, sure I must have heard that wrong. "What are you talking about?"

"Azazel said it himself." Darra stood strong, as if she wasn't talking about her own life here. "The only way you pose a threat to him is by killing a supernatural to ignite your Nephilim powers."

"But the Foster witch who cast the boundary spell might still be here," I said. "Azazel's a greater demon. He probably lied when he said she left."

"He's not lying," Camelia said.

"How do you know?"

"Because like I said earlier, I know witch history," she said. "The pure, ancient magic the Foster witches used allowed them to cast boundary spells they didn't have to be there to maintain. When I was living at the Vale, Laila was going to breed me—the strongest witch she knew—to the strongest male witch she could find. She'd been breeding witches for generations. She wanted to create a witch as strong as the Fosters had been—a witch that could make the boundary around the Vale stronger than I ever could."

Horror filled me to my core, and I searched my mind for another option. "We can't just give up," I said. "Can't we at least check to see if she's here? You can teleport around the island. Try to find her."

"The magic I'm using to keep Azazel out of this cave is extensive." Camelia's eyes were sad—I'd never seen her look so vulnerable. It was how I knew she was telling the truth. "If I teleport out, it won't hold. He'll kill you all. Then he'll find and kill me. None of us will make it off this island alive."

"Unless you're a Nephilim," Darra continued, looking straight at me. "But to become a Nephilim, you have to kill one of us to ignite your powers. Azazel doesn't think you have it in you to follow through. If he did, he wouldn't have let us be alone in here to talk. So you need to prove him wrong."

"No." I shook my head, refusing to believe it. But as I looked at Noah and Camelia, their expressions said it all.

They agreed with Darra.

"I won't do it," I said. "There has to be another way."

"You could technically kill any of the three of us." Darra spoke so casually, as if this wasn't her *life* we were talking about. "But Noah is your soul mate—I'd never ask you to harm him, nor would I expect you to. Camelia's pregnant. Her unborn child deserves a chance at life. So that leaves me."

A lump formed in my throat as I continued to look between the three of them, a chill sinking down into my bones. I couldn't accept that it was coming to this.

Why hadn't I done what I was supposed to do and killed Dr. Foster back when we'd first found him? If I hadn't been so determined to go the moral route, I wouldn't be stuck in this impossible place right now.

I'd tried so hard to do the right thing. How had it managed to go so wrong?

"I guess you don't have any spells to reverse time." I looked desperately to Camelia, clawing for any other option.

"I don't." She shook her head, pity in her eyes. "Not even the Foster witches or the mages can control time."

"I know you don't want to do this." Darra held her chin high, her gaze locked on mine. "But I promise you Raven, it's for the best. I've had a long life. I've had a *good* life. If I were human, I likely would have passed away of old age naturally by now. I'm already living on extra time. So if this is what I'm meant to do—to sacrifice myself so you can defeat Azazel and the other demons on Earth—I'm proud to do it. I *want* to do it."

"No one ever wants to die," I said.

"I'm a warrior," she replied. "I risk my life every time I enter a fight. I was training the Earth Angel's army so I could eventually lead them into battle. I've long since faced the fact that I could likely die fighting for the cause. And I couldn't wish for a better way to go than by helping you do what I've been training you to do—to become a Nephilim. It will be an honor and a privilege to be the one to ignite your powers."

From her strong, determined gaze, I knew she meant every word. Especially because Darra was never one to sugar coat the truth or hold back from sharing her thoughts.

I just didn't think I could do it. Darra was my mentor. I trusted and admired her. I wouldn't be here today if she hadn't taken me under her wing and trained me personally.

How could I possibly kill her?

I looked to Noah and reached for him with the imprint bond. We connected instantly. *What should I do?* I asked, speaking through the bond instead of out loud.

His eyes met mine, strong and determined. *This is your decision,* he said. *You have to do what feels right.*

That's not helpful. It took all of my self-control to resist rolling my eyes.

Darra isn't the only other supernatural here, he reminded me. *I'm here, too. As is Camelia.*

Are you suggesting that I kill either my soul mate or a pregnant woman? I balked at the thought of doing either of those things.

I'm just reminding you of your options.

Well, I definitely won't kill either of you, I said. *I can't.*

But you might be able to kill Darra?

I paused before responding. Because I didn't want to kill her.

But as much as I hated it, it was the most strategic way out of this mess.

"There has to be another way," I spoke out loud again, since Noah was only telling me what I already knew. He couldn't make this decision for me.

I was the only one who would have to live with what I did in this cave today.

"We can't stay in this cave forever," Darra said. "We'll either starve to death, or have to go outside for food and water. Once we venture out, Azazel will attack. Without a Nephilim, we'll be able to hold him off for a bit. But we'll eventually tire. And then he'll kill us."

"We can only beat him if I become a Nephilim," I said what we all already knew.

"Yes." Darra nodded and stepped forward, so there were only a few feet between us. "I'm proud of you, Raven. I've always believed in you, and I know you'll do what's necessary to help us win the war against the demons. No matter how hard those decisions might be."

Even if it meant killing my mentor.

Tears welled in my eyes. I couldn't believe this was happening. It was like something out of a nightmare.

"I look forward to seeing my loved ones in the Beyond." She looked up at the green sparkling lights on the ceiling and smiled wistfully, as if thinking of those before her. Then she zeroed in on me again, her mind back in the present. "On Avalon, I taught you the best ways to kill each supernatural creature," she said. "All I ask is that you honor me by giving me a quick, clean death. You know how to do that."

I stood totally still, unable to move. I hated this.

But I also knew deep in my heart that everything Darra was saying made sense.

Suddenly, a warm burst of strength filled my soul. It came from the imprint bond—from Noah.

He might not want to tell me what to do, but that gesture said everything. He knew what I needed to do just as much as I did. And he was trying to help me accept it.

I didn't think I'd ever be able to accept it.

But we'd either all die, or one of us would die. So as much as I hated this and knew I'd never be able to forgive myself for it, I knew deep down that I might be able to do it.

Too many lives were at stake for me to refuse to consider it.

"If I do this, what's to stop Azazel from teleporting off the island the moment he sees I'm a Nephilim?" I turned to Camelia, directing the question to her since she was the one with the magic.

"Once it's done and you give me the word, I'll change the boundary from one that keeps things out to one that keeps things in," she said. "Before Azazel realizes what I've done, I'll expand the boundary so he's locked in here with us. He won't be able to teleport out. But keeping the boundary strong enough to trap a greater demon will require a lot of my magic. I won't be able to hold it for long. So you'll need to take care of him as quickly as possible."

"You also need to take care of him as quickly as possible because that's the best chance you have to beat him," Darra chimed in. "You'll have angel instinct after igniting your Nephilim powers. But Azazel's stronger than you, and he has years of fighting experience on you. You have your cloaking ring on, which will keep him from immediately knowing what happened. So you'll have the element of surprise. It's imperative that you use it to your advantage and attack while he's still unaware that you're a Nephilim."

"*If* I do this at all," I said. "I never said I agreed."

"You're going to do it," she said. "You know as well as the rest of us that this is the best option. I can tell."

I said nothing. Because as much as I hated it, she was right.

She gave me a single nod, as if assuring me it was okay.

I reached for the handle of my sword, my hand shaking. "Are you ready?" I asked, my voice wavering as I spoke.

Darra squared her shoulders, looked me straight in the eyes, and said, "Yes. I'm ready."

24

RAVEN

I DREW Excalibur from my weapons belt. Flames danced around the blade the moment it was free.

Like always when I used the mystical sword, it connected with my soul, letting my body know exactly what it needed to do. My eyes met with Darra's. She nodded again, reassuring me.

If I thought about it any more, I wouldn't be able to go through with it.

So I sprinted forward and ran the flaming sword straight through her heart. I held my gaze with hers the entire time. Anything else felt like a disservice to her sacrifice.

Life disappeared from her eyes in a second.

Before I could comprehend what I'd done, white light exploded around me. An electrical jolt shot through the sword, into my hand, and through my body. Electricity buzzed through me, hot and consuming. It was like being struck by lightning.

The haze around my mind from the memory potion lifted, and my memories returned at once. They danced around in my mind as clear as ever, as if they'd never gone missing at all.

I remembered Geneva approaching me on the boardwalk as I walked home from the beach. I hadn't thought much of her strange flapper outfit at the time, since there were all kinds of unique characters on Venice Beach.

But then she'd touched me and teleported me to a dark, windowless dungeon. She'd locked me in a cell.

I remembered the others in the prison with me. The homely older woman Susan, and the glamorous vampire princess Stephenie. Susan had been in the cell next to me, and Stephenie had been across.

I remembered conversations with them that went long into the night. Mainly with Stephenie, who'd told me about the vampire kingdoms. Maybe that was why I'd been so quick in my studies at the academy. I'd already known a lot of what I was being taught. I'd simply needed a reminder.

I remembered Geneva coming in to feed me and take my blood each day to create the transformation potion.

I remembered when Susan had slit her wrists to try taking her own life, and how Geneva had used Stephenie's blood to save her.

That was how I'd known vampire blood could cure a dying human. I'd seen it with my own eyes.

I remembered when Geneva had freed us, sending Stephenie back to the Vale and bringing Susan and me to the Haven. I remembered meeting Mary and Annika there for the first time. I remembered being forced to drink the memory potion.

Afterward, Geneva had dropped me off on the boardwalk where she'd originally found me. I'd stumbled home in a confused daze, confessed to my mom that I'd taken a sudden trip to Europe, and apologized for not telling her where I'd been.

All of the memories hit me in less than a second.

And along with the sudden influx of memories, there was the sudden influx of *power*.

My senses intensified, like they had after drinking vampire blood. I could see every crack in the cave walls and hear every droplet of water as it hit the ground. I could even hear three heartbeats apart from my own. Noah's, Camelia's, and a smaller, softer one. Camelia's unborn baby.

The white glow lighting up the cave—the glow coming from *my* body—dimmed down.

I was staring straight into Darra's empty eyes.

I pulled my sword out of her chest, and her body collapsed into a heap on the ground. I dropped the sword and fell to my knees beside her. Tears flowed from my eyes, and I hung my head, letting the grief consume me.

Darra was gone. I'd killed her. She was dead because of me.

"Why is she still here?" I finally spoke, once I could breathe again. "When Noah killed the demons, they disintegrated into ashes."

"Only demons and original vampires disintegrate when killed," Camelia said. "Otherwise, witches are sent to deal with the body."

Noah walked to stand beside me and placed a hand on my shoulder. His touch was warm and welcoming, and I let myself fall into it.

I took a deep breath, overcome with the sudden influx of scents. Noah's was earthy, like I was standing in a forest of pine trees. Camelia's was sweet like flowers, with a hint of maple syrup. There was also a weaker, metallic scent. Darra's.

What was left of her, anyway. The body I was looking at was just a shell. Darra's spirit was gone.

"What do I smell like?" I asked quietly. "Now that I'm Nephilim?"

Noah kneeled down and took my hands in his, helping me stand. I didn't want to move away from Darra's body. But at the same time, I knew that wasn't Darra anymore. So I allowed him to help me up.

He stared into my eyes, looking awestruck. "You smell like honey," he said. "And your eyes… they're amazing."

"Are they like the Earth Angel's?"

"Not quite," he said. "Her eyes are bright, metallic gold. They're so gold it's jarring and unnatural. Yours are still gold, but warm. Like a burst of sunlight. They're perfect."

My cheeks heated. I knew I had to be blushing. Then I looked back down at Darra's body, and my heart fell.

How had I allowed myself even a moment of happiness after what I'd just done?

"What's going to happen to her?" I asked.

"We'll hold a funeral on Avalon," Noah said. "Like the one we had for Cassandra at the Haven."

I nodded, since it made sense. Cassandra's funeral pyre had been beautiful. After Darra's sacrifice, she deserved a hero's send off as well.

"Good," I said. "I want everyone to know what she did here today. I want them to know what she sacrificed."

"They will." Noah looked me up and down, concern

in his deep brown eyes. "But in the meantime, how do you feel?"

I took a second to contemplate the question, digging deep within my soul to make sure I answered correctly. "I feel different." I picked Excalibur back up, amazed by how perfect the weapon felt in my hand. "Stronger. There's this buzz in my veins… an ache to fight. I can feel Azazel out there. And I know I can beat him."

The bright orange flames around Excalibur's blade danced higher as I said the final part, as if the Holy Sword itself was agreeing with my statement.

Camelia stepped forward to stand across from us. The flames reflected in her eyes, and she looked ready for battle. "I'm going to expand the barrier now," she said. "It's going to be obvious when Azazel's inside. Once he is, attack immediately. Like Darra said, the sooner you attack—"

"The better my chance of winning," I completed her sentence, tightening my grip around Excalibur's handle. "I know. And I'm ready."

The crazy thing was, I meant it.

"Good." She held her hands up and stared at the foggy boundary. "Then here goes nothing."

25

RAVEN

Since Camelia was using dark magic to keep Azazel in the boundary, she used blood from the vial in her weapons belt when she did the spell.

Like before, yellow light ebbed from her hands as she chanted. She stood still, focused as she cast the spell. Keeping a greater demon inside the boundary would take all of her magic. So much of it that she wouldn't be able to help in the fight. All of her focus needed to be on keeping Azazel contained, so he wouldn't be able to teleport off the island.

The foggy boundary at the cave wall glimmered and expanded, like an inflating balloon. It passed over Azazel, until he was standing in the boundary with us.

The greater demon looked around, dazed and

confused. I supposed he hadn't been expecting the boundary to expand to include him.

This was my chance.

I ran at him, sword flaming, aiming for his heart.

I was fast. But so was he.

Before I could blink, he was also holding a sword, and it clanged with mine. He growled at me, his eyes glowing red, and swung the sword aggressively in my direction.

Instinct took over—it must have been the angel instinct Darra had said I'd get upon becoming Nephilim —and I expertly blocked each swing. Some of them came dangerously close to piercing my skin, but I managed to hold him off each time.

It was easy.

Until he caught me off guard and hit Excalibur so hard that he knocked it out of my hand and across the cave.

Panic rushed through me as I glanced at the fallen weapon. I *needed* Excalibur.

Just like that, the Holy Sword flared back to life, flew through the air, and smacked straight back into my palm. I gripped it tightly, moving it in front of me just in time to stop Azazel from taking a fatal blow at my chest.

He roared with anger, backing me up so I was pressed against the wall of the cave. He used his strength to push my flaming sword closer and closer to my neck. I grunted as I pushed back at him, using all my might to stop him from forcing my sword to slice off my own head.

"You did it." He laughed, giving me a full view of his pointed yellow teeth. "I didn't think you had the balls to go through with killing the vampire. But it doesn't change the fact that you're, young, weak, and inexperienced. Too bad she'll have died for nothing."

He snarled and put his full body strength into the weight of his sword. My muscles quivered. Like Darra had warned, he was bigger and stronger than me. I didn't know how much longer I could hold him off.

No matter how hard I pushed back, I couldn't get him to move an inch. Sweat formed at my brow, threatening to drip into my eyes. I wasn't sure if it was from my weakening muscles, or from the heat of Excalibur's flames. Probably both.

"I'll be sure to tell your mother all the gory details about how you died." He smiled, clearly getting joy from this. "Although I'm sure she already knows, since she foresaw it and sent me here to finish you off herself."

I glared at him. It had to be lies. My mom would never betray me like that.

He pushed down harder, and my arm lowered further. I winced as the flames brushed my neck, burning the skin they touched. Only a few millimeters left until my blade would cut into my skin.

Suddenly, someone leaped at Azazel from behind. Noah, in his wolf form. His powerful, deadly jaws clamped around Azazel's neck, his front claws digging into his shoulders to pull the greater demon off of me.

Azazel's red eyes turned bloodshot and practically popped out of their sockets. He snarled and used his free hand to try wrangling Noah off of him.

No longer cornered against the wall, I could kill Azazel now. But he and Noah moved fast as they wrestled each other. With Azazel so entwined with Noah, I couldn't find an opening that would guarantee Noah remained unharmed.

"Do it!" Camelia screamed. "Now!"

She was right. This was my chance.

But I couldn't take a swing at Azazel if it meant possibly killing Noah in the process.

It took some prying, but Azazel managed to throw Noah to the ground. I heard two snaps as his hind legs broke. Bone popped through his skin. Through the imprint bond, I felt an echo of his pain.

The bite and claw marks on Azazel's skin healed in seconds. I went in and swung at him with Excalibur, but the greater demon fended me off, his sword clanging with mine.

Noah also recovered quickly. His legs set back in place, and he stood up, backing up and running to pounce at Azazel again. He opened his deadly jaw, ready to attack.

Azazel snarled, apparently not going to fall for the same trick twice. This time, as Noah flew through the air, Azazel shoved me to the ground with his foot, turning around and raising his sword to slice my future mate in two.

Azazel was fast. But now that I was a Nephilim, I was faster. And by turning away for only a split second, the greater demon had underestimated me.

Because before he could swing down at Noah, I rushed toward Azazel, running Excalibur through his back and straight into his heart.

26

RAVEN

AZAZEL FROZE, like he'd turned to stone the moment Excalibur pierced his heart. Spidery black lines traveled outward from where my blade had entered his chest, crawling up his neck and extending all the way out to the tips of his fingers. The black expanded until it covered every inch of his skin.

Then he crumbled to dust, clothes and all.

The only remains in the pile of ash were his yellowed, pointy teeth.

I'd done it. I'd killed a greater demon. And not just any greater demon. I'd killed *Azazel*.

Since my sword was now paused in mid-air, I slid it back into my weapons belt. But the motion was stiff and robotic. I couldn't stop staring at the pile of ashes at my feet.

At some point while I was staring at the ashes, Noah had shifted back into human form. He stepped up beside me and reached for my hand, clasping it in his.

"You did it," he said, his eyes glowing with love. "He's gone."

"Sage is free." The shock disappeared, and I jumped to what came next. Because even though Azazel was dead, my mission wasn't over. "And my mom. Azazel sounded like he had my mom with him. Probably at the Montgomery compound, where he was staying with the blood bound shifters. We have to go there. Now." I looked frantically at Camelia, since she was our best hope at getting there.

The pregnant witch was just standing there, observing us. "What are you looking at me for?" she asked, crossing her arms in annoyance.

"You can teleport." I wanted to strangle her for being so dense. But I stopped myself, since I needed her alive and functioning so she could use her magic. I also couldn't risk hurting the baby. "You can take us to the Montgomery compound."

"Do you listen to anything I say?" She huffed, clearly fed up with me, even though I was Nephilim and not a human anymore. "I can't leave Avalon or its satellite islands."

"You can't?" I challenged. "Or you won't?"

From what she'd told us earlier, it sounded like leaving Avalon and its surrounding islands was just something she was *afraid* to do because of whatever deal she'd made with the fae. Not something she *couldn't* do.

"I won't," she said.

"Yeah, well I didn't *want* to kill Darra to ignite my Nephilim powers, but I did it because I had no other choice." I stomped toward her, my hair blowing behind me like I was a goddess on a rampage. The rage I felt toward her was like an inferno building in my chest, and I made no effort to contain the blaze. "We know from the bunker that Azazel has demon minions working for him," I continued. "They could be at the Montgomery compound right now. Once they realize the demon bond is broken, they'll know Azazel's dead. And who knows what they'll do to my mom, and Sage, and the others then?" My heart pounded in panic just from thinking about it. "If anything happens to them, and it's because *you* were afraid to leave the Avalon borders to get us there fast enough, it'll be your fault."

Camelia continued staring at me, blinking slowly.

I had a terrible feeling from her hollow gaze that she didn't care what happened to my mom, or to Sage, or to any of the wolf shifters who had been demon bound and were now getting their free will returned to them.

My blood pounded faster through my veins. I itched

to take Excalibur back out and show her who was boss. My newly ignited Nephilim side urged me to use force to convince Camelia to help me save my family and friends.

But I wouldn't be able to live with myself if anything I did hurt the unborn child. So I clenched my fists to my sides and reined it in. For the child's sake.

From the way Noah was snarling and bearing his teeth at Camelia, I suspected he was experiencing the same inner turmoil that I was. Or maybe we were both feeling the other's emotions through the imprint bond. We were so connected by now that it was hard to tell.

"I'll teleport you back to Avalon so the witches there can bring you to the Montgomery compound." Camelia walked up to us and took our hands in hers. "It'll take extra strength to teleport two people, but because of the added strength from the pregnancy, I can do it. Are you ready?"

"What about Darra?" I glanced at my mentor's body, lying in a heap near the wall of the cave. Leaving her there, cold and alone, felt so wrong.

"Once we're on Avalon, I'll send witches to come get her," Camelia said. "We'll have a funeral pyre for her once you're back from your mission to the Montgomery compound."

I nodded, unsure what to say. What had happened to

Darra was awful. When I saw her twin sister Tari again… how could I ever break the news to her?

Just thinking about it made me feel like I was falling apart all over again.

"Thank you." Noah spoke for me, since I was too emotional to find the words. "We'll give her a pyre she deserves."

Camelia made a noise of agreement. Then her eyes went blank, and I braced myself for the sudden displacement that always occurred while teleporting.

But nothing happened.

"What are you waiting for?" I asked, impatient to get to my mom and Sage. "Let's go."

"I can't." Camelia blinked, stunned. "The spell that the Foster witch cast around this island is still in place."

The hope in my chest deflated. "What do we do then?" I asked. Because even though I was a Nephilim, I couldn't teleport. Only witches, mages, angels, and greater demons had that ability.

"We can try getting to the edge of the boundary spell," Camelia said. "Foster magic is strong, but thanks to my pregnancy, I'm stronger than ever. If I get close enough to touch the boundary, I can see if there's anything I can do to break us through."

27

RAVEN

THE BOUNDARY SPELL went beyond the land and out to the sea.

So the three of us trekked back to where we'd hidden the sailboat. Now that I was Nephilim, we got there in a fraction of the time it had taken us before, since I could now move at supernatural speed too. And I had to say—running through the trees as a supernatural felt *good*.

It didn't take us long to uncover the boat. We carried it out of the jungle, across the beach, and to the ocean. Well, Noah and I did the heavy lifting, thanks to Camelia's condition. Camelia just watched and brushed her hair with her fingers, like a spoiled princess.

Luckily, the "heavy lifting," wasn't heavy at all, thanks to my newly acquired supernatural strength. Carrying the boat was so easy that if anyone had been looking on, they would have thought we were carrying a foam prop instead of the real thing.

After being a weak human that needed constant protection for so long, it felt amazing to finally be useful. I couldn't wait to get to the Montgomery compound and show those demons what I was made of.

Excalibur buzzed at my side, as if the Holy Sword was supporting my desire for revenge.

The three of us were quiet once we set sail, the air between us thick with worry. And I knew why.

It was because Camelia wasn't sure she could break past this boundary. We were holding onto hope that she could, and we wanted to *believe* she could. Especially because she seemed to think it was possible. And while Camelia had her fair share of grandiose thoughts, she also didn't seem like the type of person to sugar coat the truth.

I supposed she was kind of like Darra in that way.

But there was still the chance that whatever Camelia planned on doing to break through the boundary wouldn't work.

If that happened, where would it leave us?

I bit my lip in worry, trying not to imagine the worst. Because all we could do now was sail on.

Eventually, the tip of the sailboat hit an invisible wall. The boundary.

I walked to the front of the boat and pressed my hands against the barrier. It was so strange. Even though we were in the middle of the ocean, it felt like holding my hands up to glass. Except the "glass" was invisible.

"So," I said, glancing back at Camelia. "Are you ready to break through?"

"You bet I am." She made her way to the front of the boat, and I moved aside to give her room.

It was amazing that her pregnancy wasn't holding her back, besides an occasional pause when she'd rest a hand on her stomach.

She stared at the invisible wall, held out her palms, and started chanting in Latin. The yellow glow of her magic emanated from her palms and touched the surface of the boundary. It glowed brighter and brighter, until it was so bright that I had to shield my eyes. It burned even more intensely than before, thanks to my new supernatural senses. Noah shielded his eyes, too.

She stopped chanting, and the glow dimmed. The spell was done.

Figuring it was safe to look without getting blinded, I lowered my arm from my eyes.

Everything looked the same as before.

"Did it work?" I asked.

The tip of the boat hit the invisible boundary again, squashing my hopes.

"No." She glared at the wall and backed away from it. "The Foster witches are too strong. I can't break through."

Noah bared his teeth at her. "Can you try again?" he asked, although it sounded more like an order than a question. "And put more magic into it this time."

"Even with the boost from my pregnancy, my magic isn't infinite." Camelia sat down in the center of the boat and rested a hand on her stomach. "And I've used a lot of it today. I have to wait to recharge."

"How long will that take?" he asked.

"I can try again in a few hours," she said. "But I'll need a full twenty-four hours if I want my magic working at full capacity."

"We don't have twenty-four hours." I rushed to the front of the boat, pressed my hands against the boundary again, and pushed. Nothing happened. "We need to get out of here now."

Panic coursed through my veins. My breaths came shorter and shallower—it was hard to get air into my lungs. I had to escape this island. I needed to get out. My mom, Sage, and the others… they needed me.

As I looked around like a trapped bird, the energy built and built inside of me, begging for release. If I didn't release it, I feared I might explode from the intensity of it all.

And so, I pulled Excalibur out of my weapons belt, raised it high above my head, and crashed it down *hard* against the invisible wall.

The electricity from my body poured through the sword, straight into the wall.

Sparks flew where the blade hit the boundary, electricity expanding outward from the point of the sword. The boundary was shaped like a dome, and the entire thing lit up with spidery bolts that looked like lightning. It was so bright that the surrounding ocean and the island behind us glowed with the unnatural blue light. Wind rushed around me, but I kept Excalibur pressed against the boundary, energy buzzing from my body and out through the blade. The energy inside of me drew power from itself, endless and infinite.

I wasn't just *using* magic. I *was* the magic.

The electricity lighting up the dome expanded outward until it was no longer shaped like bolts. Now, the entire dome glowed blue. It crackled and buzzed, getting brighter and brighter by the second. It got so bright that it burned, like it was the sun itself. But I kept my eyes open despite the pain, determined to see what was happening.

There was a giant popping sound, accompanied by

the smell of something burning. Then the light shut off completely. It was like someone had turned off a switch.

Even though it was daytime, it looked dark in comparison to the bright glow from moments before. Water lapped against the sides of the boat as it bobbed in the ocean, but other than that, everything was eerily silent.

Suddenly, Excalibur slid through where the wall had been. I widened my eyes and reached forward with my other hand, needing to make sure this was really happening.

Nothing stopped it.

"I think I did it." I let my sword hang to my side and turned to Noah and Camelia. They were both staring at me with equally shocked expressions. "I destroyed the boundary."

28

SAGE

I WAS SITTING on my favorite swing off by the side of the compound, making designs in the dirt with my toes under the star filled nighttime sky, when the haze lifted.

One moment, my mind was hazy and muddled. It was like being surrounded by fog and blinded by it.

The next, all was clear again.

I blinked and gripped the chains of the swing. Some of my other pack members were in the yard, too. They'd also stopped what they'd been doing, and were now looking around, dazed and confused.

The last I remembered, I was standing in a circle with my pack in the center of the compound. Azazel had been there, along with the Foster witch. Lavinia.

Azazel had made us drink his blood from a goblet, and Lavinia had lit up the night with a spell.

Then it was like something had taken over my body. A will that wasn't my own. I'd been a prisoner, trapped and watching myself do things through my own eyes, unable to stop myself.

As I sat there, my toes motionless in the dirt as I let the memories pour through me, I remembered it all. Every awful second of it.

Most of all, I remembered the anguished look in Thomas's eyes when I'd told him to get lost. He'd come to rescue me, and I'd been apathetic and cruel to him.

I hated myself for it.

But I hated Azazel, Mara, and Lavinia even more.

I stood up from the swing, determined to find the Foster witch. I couldn't kill a greater demon since I wasn't Nephilim, and I didn't have a holy weapon to kill Mara. But Lavinia was fair game. And she had it coming for her.

I focused on the guesthouse, since that was where Lavinia had been living. My wolf form ached to burst out, run into the house to find her, claw her skin to shreds, and wrangle her throat with my jaw and teeth. I'd make her death long and painful. She deserved every excruciating second of it.

But someone appeared next to me and placed a hand on my arm, stopping me in my tracks. A woman with deep brown skin and caring eyes, wearing white pants and a matching shirt. She looked like she'd popped in from a new age yoga retreat. She wore a cloaking ring, which was why she had no scent. I only knew she was a witch because she'd teleported here.

"Please don't panic," she whispered, so quietly that my pack mates across the yard wouldn't hear her. "I'm here to help you."

I stilled and remained on guard, ready to attack at any moment despite my instincts telling me to trust her. "Who are you?" I asked, keeping my voice equally as low.

"My name is Shivani," she said. "I'm a witch from the Haven. Rosella, our trusted vampire seer, sent me here. She told me to give you this."

She pulled her other hand out from around her back, producing a gleaming silver longsword with a black onyx handle.

I took the sword from her and examined it. "What's so special about this sword?" I asked, since it *had* to be special, for a Haven witch to come all the way here to give it to me.

"This is the holy weapon the Earth Angel used to slay the greater demon Samael after the Hell Gate was opened in the Vale," she explained, and suddenly, the sword felt much heavier in my hand. Mind blown, I remained silent as she continued, "It was turned into a holy weapon in Heaven by the angel Emmanuel himself.

After the Earth Angel killed Samael, she gifted the sword to Mary for safekeeping. Rosella instructed that I give this sword to you, at this exact location, at this precise moment in time. She also instructed me to leave immediately afterward. But not without first reminding you that any supernatural who needs a safe place on Earth is always welcome at the Haven."

With that, she flashed out, leaving me alone with the sword.

And not just *any* sword.

This was the holy weapon the Earth Angel had used to slay the greater demon Samael.

Holy crap. I didn't know what I'd done to deserve being gifted such an incredible weapon, but I was going to use it wisely.

Which meant it was time to kick some demon ass.

29

SAGE

WHILE I'D BEEN in the shadows talking with Shivani, some of my pack mates had already oriented themselves and started attacking the demon guards.

But without holy weapons, they couldn't kill the demons. They'd shifted and were clawing and going at them with their jaws. My pack mates were holding their own, but no matter what they did, the demons wouldn't die.

Closest to me, Linden shifted and pounced on a demon. He managed to get a few swipes in with his claws, but the demon seemed more annoyed by the attack than anything.

I rushed forward to help him. But before I got there, the demon sliced at Linden with his sword, separating his head from his body. Linden's head rolled, his body collapsing to the ground. Both parts of him returned to human form upon his death.

Pain burst through me, as always happened when a pack mate died. Linden was a jerk and we butted heads a lot, but we were still pack.

His death left an empty spot in my heart that would never be filled.

Charged with rage, I rushed toward the demon that had killed Linden, my sword held high. The demon was taller and bigger than I was, but I had stealth and speed on my side.

He countered my blows with his own, our blades clashing against each other. My anger at the demons grew with every clang of our blades. He pushed me back with his strength, but I ducked and jumped away every time he went in for a fatal swing.

His red eyes burned with anger, and he growled, as if he didn't understand why I wasn't dead yet.

Amused by his frustration, I smiled at him. Training with Noah for all those months had taught me well.

Finally, the demon started slowing down. He was a second too late with stopping my next blow, and my sword passed his, going straight through his chest and into his heart.

His eyes widened and he disintegrated into a pile of ash and teeth.

Adrenaline coursed through my veins. For months, I'd helped Noah hold the demons off, always watching when he gave the final killing blow.

This was the first time I'd done it myself.

It felt incredible.

But I had no time to celebrate my victory. Because my other pack mates were still fighting demons in the yard. The strongest fighters had taken up the lead, and were holding their own. But without holy weapons to kill the demons, it didn't matter how good of fighters they were. They needed my help.

I glanced around, looking for Lavinia. But she was nowhere to be found. Disappointing, but probably for the best. Because my pack mates could take her on. With my newly gifted holy weapon, I needed to fight where I was needed the most.

Against the demons.

And so, I rushed toward the closest demon, jumping in and helping with the fight. It was harder to fight while going two against one—you needed to be hyper aware of everything happening around you as to not harm the person on your side—but wolves were wired to hunt in packs. Plus, I'd gotten better at it while fighting with Noah.

Once I found my in, I killed this demon just like I'd killed the first.

The pack mate I'd been fighting with—Dale—stared at my sword in amazement. He shifted his head back to human form so he could speak. "Where did you get that?" he asked.

"A Haven witch dropped by and gave it to me." I smirked, not explaining more before hurrying over to help out with the next demon.

My pack mates backed me up as I fought demon by demon. Flint fought at the opposite side of the compound. He was holding his own, but I kept my distance for now. What he'd done by forcing our pack to bind ourselves to the demons... it was unforgivable.

But I couldn't think about my anger toward him now. I needed to concentrate on killing demons. One at a time. It was taking a level of strength and focus I hadn't needed until now. But I could do this. I *had* to do this.

At least, I was trying to do it. I'd taken down four demons so far, and was battling it out with a fifth. He was taking longer than the others. I was fine doing this myself—I wasn't one to back down, and I had a lot to fight for—but it would have been nice if we had more than one holy weapon at our disposal.

"Keep going!" I called out to my other pack mates. They hadn't given up, but they were tiring. Linden hadn't been the only death—Jean had been lost too—but there was no time to grieve. We needed to stay focused. "Hold them off until I get to you!"

That was what they'd needed to hear, and they howled intermittently—a battle cry against the demons that had been controlling us for months.

I howled too, despite being in human form so I could use my sword. It wasn't as loud as a howl from a shifted wolf, but it sent a burst of power through me all the same.

Just as I shoved my sword through the demon's heart, six people teleported into the center of the yard.

Raven, Noah, Bella, two witches I didn't recognize... and Thomas.

Our eyes met, and my heart swelled at the sight of him.

He ran toward me, and the world slowed. But as he got closer, he reached for his longsword, held it forward, and swung.

He hit something right behind me.

I turned around just in time to see that his sword had pierced a demon's heart. The demon disintegrated into a pile of ash and teeth at our feet.

"You were so enraptured by my presence that you failed to notice the demon trying to kill you from behind." Thomas smirked and stepped closer to me, so there was barely any space between us. "Understandable. I tend to have that effect on people."

As I stared up at him, so many thoughts rushed through my mind at once. I missed him. I was sorry for everything I'd said to him when he'd tried rescuing me. I was an idiot for thinking he'd never cared about me for all those years. I loved him. I wanted to make that love official and become mates.

My imprint bond warmed, making me hopeful that he knew what I was thinking despite the fact that it was too much to put into words right now.

From the intense way he stared down at me, I knew he'd felt every thought.

My stomach warmed under his loving, protective gaze. I wanted to take him in my arms and make him mine *now*.

But we were in the middle of a battle. My pack mates needed us. And I assumed he and the others were here—with more holy weapons—to help us fight.

"Come on," I said instead, holding up my sword and matching his smirk with one of my own. "We have demons to kill."

30

RAVEN

ONCE NOAH, Thomas, Bella, the other two witches who had teleported us, and I arrived at the Montgomery compound with our holy weapons, we jumped in to help the wolves fight the demon guards.

Sage had been holding strong so far with a holy weapon of her own. I had no idea how she'd gotten one, but I was glad for it. Many more wolves would have been dead already otherwise.

Now, it felt amazing to fight alongside my friends instead of watching from the sidelines. As Excalibur sliced through the air, flames dancing around the blade as I swung and attacked, it felt like this was what I'd always been meant to do.

It didn't take long before all the demons in the yard were piles of ash.

I wanted to run up to Sage and tell her how glad I was that she was okay. But just because there were no more demons in the yard didn't mean we were in the clear. So I couldn't let my guard down just yet.

"I smell another one in the main house," Noah said. "Raven and I will take that one. The rest of you—check the rest of the premises and take care of any other demons you find. We'll meet back here once the compound is clear."

Sage nodded and led Thomas toward the guesthouse. Judging from the way she hurried, she had a score to settle with someone in there.

Noah and I entered the main house. It looked almost the same as it had the last time I'd been there—when Noah had first brought me there after saving me from Eli and Azazel in the alley.

But now I was accosted with the smells of all kinds of supernatural creatures. Mainly the woodsy smell of shifters, but also the burnt smell of demons and the metallic scent of vampires. There was also a barely noticeable smell of sickly sweetness—a dark witch. It was so faint that I suspected the witch was long gone.

As we went up the stairs, the smell of demon, vampire, and a hint of shifter got stronger. My Nephilim senses tuned me into the direction it was coming from —the master bedroom.

I threw open the doors, and my eyes met with familiar green ones I'd recognize anywhere.

"Mom!" I gasped, my eyes welling with tears at the sight of her.

She looked just as I remembered. Red hair just like mine, but cut shorter. But she was also paler. The lines of her cheeks and face were harsher and more defined, like she'd been airbrushed for a magazine. And she smelled metallic... like a vampire.

Azazel had said my mom was now a vampire. But demons lied. It was one thing to hear it, and another to see it and know it was true.

But we couldn't have our big reunion just yet. Because there was a demon standing right next to my mom. A blonde, petite demon who quivered at the sight of me and had a slight smell of shifter on her, but a demon nonetheless.

I raised Excalibur and rushed toward the demon, ready to make the kill.

But my mom jumped in front of her, protecting her.

I pulled myself to a stop a second before Excalibur touched my mom. That was close. *Too* close.

I tried to go around my mom to get to the demon. But now that my mom was a vampire, she was fast enough to block my every move.

"Get out of my way," I growled, my voice sounding

way more intimidating than I'd planned. My mom needed to let me take care of this demon so we could get out of here.

"Please, stop." My mom held her arms out, her eyes begging me to listen.

I narrowed my eyes at her. My angel instinct wanted me to fight.

But because this was my mom, I reined in my urge to attack. If she were any other vampire—or if I were any other Nephilim—I suspected she might have been dead right now along with the demon.

"She's a demon," I said, glaring at the blonde with hate. "I'm here to save you from her."

"I don't need saving from her," my mom said. "Mara's the reason you're here right now. She's the reason you're still alive. She helped me save you. Put down the sword and hear us out. Please."

Us? I looked back and forth between them in confusion, still holding tightly onto Excalibur. It almost sounded like my mom and this demon girl—Mara—were a team.

That couldn't be possible. Demons didn't team up with non-demons. Controlled and manipulated them, yes. But teamed up? Never.

"What are you talking about?" I asked.

"Will you put down the sword?" she repeated. "It's

hard to have a conversation with that thing waving in my face."

My mom had never been the violent type. She was into peace, love, and all that jazz. Apparently, becoming a vampire hadn't changed that part of her.

I continued to glance between my mom and the demon. I didn't want to put down my sword. No way was I giving this demon a chance to attack. She might look like a sweet blonde on the outside, but demons were evil to the core. I wouldn't be fooled by one.

Mara must have done a seriously good job of getting into my mom's head if my mom was protecting her like this.

"Mara won't hurt you," my mom said, her voice calmer and steadier now. It was the same voice she'd used to calm me down whenever I'd thrown tantrums as a kid. "She's on our side."

"She's a demon," Noah spoke up from next to me. He also held his weapon—his slicer—at the ready. "Demons don't care about anyone but themselves. Whatever she told you to make you think otherwise, don't believe her."

"I mated with Flint," Mara finally spoke up, wringing her hands together in front of her as she spoke. She sounded young and innocent. Not demon-like at all.

It was probably part of the game she was playing. I

could see how someone could be fooled. She was pretty convincing.

"Sage's brother?" I asked, even though there was no other Flint she could be referring to. "The alpha of the Montgomery pack?"

"Yes," Mara said, and I lowered my sword slightly, although I was still ready to strike at a moment's notice. "Mating with him changed me. It gave me a conscience. And ever since then, nothing in my life has been the same."

31

RAVEN

MARA and my mom quickly told us about how much Mara had changed, including her new ability to shift into a wolf. Noah came to the same conclusion that Mara had—she was a dyad.

By mating with Flint, their souls had melded, and she'd developed a conscience.

The entire story was pretty convincing. Then again, demons were skilled liars. I wished I had Jessica with me, or a vial of truth potion. But I'd come here so quickly from Avalon that I hadn't had time to pack up my weapons belt.

"Why should I believe any of this?" I asked, still holding Excalibur at the ready.

"You don't have to believe her," my mom said. "But you should believe me. You see, Mara and I have been working together for months. I've been helping her learn to accept and control her new emotions. It's been difficult, given that the demon bond on Flint put Mara in a tough situation. The bond took away Flint's free will. It took away everything that made him the man she loved. And it could only be broken by Azazel's death. It would have been an intense moral dilemma for someone who's had emotions for their entire life, let alone someone who's still adjusting to them."

I looked at Mara, seeing the demon girl in a new light. "The only way to get back your soul mate was for your father to die," I said softly.

She nodded, her eyes pained at my words. They were red like a demon's, but they weren't empty. There was actual emotion in there. There was more than pain. There was intense anguish.

Mara had been to Hell and back. Both literally and figuratively.

I wouldn't wish her problem on my greatest enemy. Well, maybe I would. But as much as it surprised me, I wasn't seeing Mara as the enemy anymore. At least, not completely.

"I chose Flint," she choked out, focused on me. "My father wanted me alive, because to him, family represents power. But he didn't love me. My time spent here with Skylar taught me what parental love *should* be like.

I'd never had that with my father. Because of what he was, he would never have been able to love me. But Flint loved me before being bound to my father, and I know he loves me now that the bond is broken. Once I knew Flint's love, I could never live without it. So I chose my mate over my father. It was the hardest decision I've ever made. But it was the right one. Because in the end, I chose love. And I'll never regret it."

I stepped closer to Noah, our imprint bond pulsing with warmth between us. As much as I didn't want to trust Mara, I understood where she was coming from. Now that I knew what the love of an imprint bond felt like, my life would be hollow if I ever lost that connection.

Mara's decision to turn on her father, as twisted as it was, made sense.

"After a few weeks of your mother being here, my father trusted me to guard her," Mara continued, looking relieved that I was listening. "I gave her a glass of blood and a dose of complacent potion twice a day. He used the complacent potion on her so she could only do tarot readings and predict the future for him. But to save Flint, I needed her to read the cards for *me*.

"So I stopped giving her the complacent potion. Instead of dosing her like I was supposed to, I flushed the potion down the toilet. No one knew the difference.

Especially because your mom played along, telling my father the truth of what she saw in the cards so he wouldn't realize anything was amiss. Up until..." She paused, her voice wavering, as if she couldn't bring herself to keep going.

"Up until the most recent tarot reading I did for Azazel." My mom stepped forward, and I lowered my sword completely. "Once Azazel forced the location of Avalon from Kara, he asked me to tell him the best tactic he could use to destroy Avalon. He believed I was on complacent potion and had no choice but to follow his command. So I did a tarot reading. But in my mind, I didn't ask the cards to tell me how he could best destroy Avalon. I asked them to show me the best way to destroy *Azazel*."

"The cards showed me killing him, didn't they?" I glanced at Excalibur, which I now held by my side. "With this."

"Yes." My mom smiled proudly. "I drew the Ace of Swords, and saw how to send Azazel to his death. I wouldn't have been able to do that without Mara's help."

"So what am I supposed to do?" I looked at the demon girl curiously. "Just... let her go?"

My angel instinct urged me not to do that. But my human instinct—something that was still a part of me, despite my transformation into a Nephilim—wanted me to trust my mom and have compassion for Mara.

"I want to go to Avalon." Mara straightened, holding my gaze with hers. "With Flint."

I stilled, since that wasn't what I was expecting her to say. "You're a demon," I said, as if she needed reminding. "You'll never be allowed onto Avalon."

That was why Arthur's simulation existed. To keep demons, and all those who didn't deserve entrance to Avalon, off the island.

"That's not true," my mom said. "Mara and Flint will pass the simulation and be allowed to live together on Avalon. I've seen it in the cards."

"And neither of them will turn on us once they get there?"

"Would Arthur let them through the simulation if they weren't deserving?" my mom replied with a question of her own.

"No," I admitted, although it didn't make me happy to say it.

I still had my doubts about how much I could trust a demon, no matter how sincere Mara seemed. But I trusted my mom, I trusted Arthur, and I trusted the magic of Avalon. For now, that was going to have to be enough.

So I placed Excalibur back inside its sheath, ran up to my mom, and enveloped her in a hug.

She hugged me back, as strong as ever. I guess that made sense, since she was a vampire and I was a Nephilim.

"I missed you," I said. "I'm so glad you're okay."

"I missed you too." She pulled back and looked into my eyes, as if she were seeing me in a new light. I supposed she was, since my eyes were gold now, and not the green they'd been before. "I've always felt you had a great destiny. You fought me on it for long enough, but I'm glad you've come into your own. I'm so proud of you, Raven. It's a mother's dream to see the strong, powerful woman you've grown to be. And you're going to continue doing great things. I know it."

I'd dreamed about being reunited with my mom for so long that this didn't feel real. Well, it did, and it didn't. There was a part of me that worried it wouldn't last.

But for now, I'd done what I'd set out to do. Azazel was dead. My mom and I were alive and together again.

Happiness and relief overcame me.

And so, for the first time in a long time, I let my guard down and cried.

SAGE

LAVINIA WAS GONE. She must have teleported out of the compound once she'd realized the blood bond was broken.

I'd hoped she'd have the guts to fight. But her departure didn't surprise me. As strong of a dark witch as she was, even she didn't want to go up against the Montgomery pack alone.

She might be safe for now. But the entire pack was out for her blood. Someday—and I didn't know when that day would be—she had it coming.

And I intended for her death to be by my hand.

Once all the demon guards on the premises were confirmed dead, we all met back in the yard. There were also two vampires with us—Derrick and Kara. Now that Azazel was dead, and he was the one to give them commands under the complacent potion, they were no longer bound to follow his orders. The complacent potion was still in their systems, but it would be gone soon enough. As long as none of us gave them any commands—which we didn't—their will was their own again.

Derrick was cool and collected, as always. Kara, not so much. The young vampire screamed and demanded to be taken back to her family. It took Derrick plus two of my other pack mates—the two most submissive pack members who were good at dealing with emotions—to get Kara under control.

Now that the battle was over and the compound was secure, I finally approached Flint.

The others formed a circle around us, watching us.

My brother stood strong and proud, although I could tell by his silence that he wasn't sure what to say to me. I didn't blame him. What could he possibly say to make amends for allying with Azazel, capturing me, and forcing the pack to go through a blood binding spell with a greater demon?

Even if I were someday able to forgive him, I'd never look at him the same way.

However, that wasn't what bothered me the most.

What bothered me most was that his eyes were still demonic red.

When the blood bond with Azazel broke, the red disappeared from my eyes, and the eyes of all the other members of the Montgomery pack. But not Flint's. His were the same as before.

He had a slight smoky smell of demon to him, too.

Had the spell been stronger and more binding for him, since he was our alpha? Was he lost to us forever?

"Your blood bond isn't broken," I accused, holding my sword to my side. Despite how furious I was about what he'd done, he was still my brother and I didn't want to use it on him. But I was ready if I had to. "You're still connected to the demons."

"I'm not," Flint said. "I don't know why my eyes are still red. But I can assure you, my bond is broken."

I narrowed my eyes at him. "Why should I believe you?"

"Because I'm your brother."

"Not good enough." I circled him, each word venomous and full of anger. "Your eyes are red. You smell like demon. You might be my brother, but I don't trust a word that comes out of your mouth." I turned to Bella and the other two Avalon witches who had come to help us fight. "Take him to the Vale," I commanded, since as the vampire kingdom of North America, the Vale upheld supernatural laws in the United States. "Let them decide what to do with him from here."

"Wait!" someone yelled, bursting out of the main house and into the yard. Mara.

Raven, Noah, and Skylar followed behind her. Raven and Noah had their swords raised to protect the young demon.

Even as Mara stepped between Flint and me, Raven and Noah remained by her sides, guarding her.

"Why are you protecting Azazel's daughter?" I asked, looking skeptically at my two best friends. I trusted them, but this made no sense.

"Flint is no longer bound to my father," Mara pleaded, sounding desperate. "His will is entirely his own. His eyes are still red and he has a slight scent of demon on him because of his mate bond with me."

"Mara." When Flint looked at his mate, his eyes were pained and broken. I'd never seen him so vulnerable, ever. "I'm so, so sorry."

"I know." She stepped toward him and took his hands in hers. "I love you. Everything I did was for you. I helped Skylar and Raven defeat my father for *you*."

He pulled her in for a kiss, and we all watched, stunned. Except for Raven, Skylar, and Noah. The three of them seemed to know exactly what was going on.

Bella stepped forward, fierce as always in her killer black heels and even deadlier sword. She pointed its tip toward Mara. "One of you better explain this before I turn blondie here to dust," she said to Skylar, Raven, and Noah.

Quickly, Skylar summarized everything she'd been up to with Mara for the past few months. The entire pack listened to the prophetess, more and more shocked with each word.

Thomas looked at Mara with the most suspicion of all of us. "If you can truly shift into a wolf, prove it," he said.

"All right." Mara stepped forward and gulped nervously. "I've yet to complete a full shift, so this won't be as graceful as you're used to seeing. But I'll do my best."

I nodded for her to go ahead.

Her hands shifted first, her fingers turning into claws. That was always the easiest part of the shift—the part we mastered upon puberty, when the witch spells that bound our animal sides were removed so we could learn to shift safely. The law insisted that shifters living amongst humans had the spell done to their young. Shifters in the wild used no such spells—they simply started shifting from birth. It would be too difficult for them to survive in the wild otherwise.

Her feet shifted next, followed by her legs and arms. The rest of her body followed, finished by her head. The shift was relatively graceful for a first time. I suspected it was because she'd been suppressing her wolf for so many months, and it was happy to be free.

Where she'd been standing was now a beautiful, golden haired wolf with startling red eyes.

We all stared at her in silence. But Flint looked most awestruck by Mara's wolf form of us all.

"Very well." Thomas was the first to speak. "You've proven your point. Now please shift back so we can continue our conversation."

Mara did as instructed, although her shift back to human form took a bit longer and was more piecemeal. Once she was human again, Flint stepped up to her, wrapped an arm protectively around her, and murmured something in her ear for only her to hear.

"So, Mara's a dyad now," Bella said. "But she's still a demon. And Flint's now a wolf/demon dyad—whatever that means for him. The supernatural community has never dealt with anything like this before. It's unprecedented. Sage is right that they should be taken to the Vale so King Alexander and the vampire court can decide what to do with them."

A few people muttered behind her in agreement. Then they looked to me. As the beta of the pack, the decision about the fate of our alpha in a situation like this was mine.

But Skylar jumped in before I could give the official

okay.

"My tarot cards have foreseen Flint and Mara being accepted onto Avalon," she said. "They'll join the Earth Angel's army. We're to let King Arthur judge them—not King Alexander. And he will judge them as worthy."

Vampire prophetesses like Skylar and Rosella were some of the most respected and revered beings in the supernatural world. So over the past few months on the compound, Skylar had earned respect from the Montgomery pack. It showed in the way we all lowered our guard at her news and listened.

Now, my pack all looked to me—their beta—for my final decision.

I couldn't send him to the Vale after our prophetess said he belonged on Avalon. But there *was* something else I could do.

Something I needed to do.

I sheathed my sword and focused on Flint. "You failed our pack." I did my best to block all emotions and stand strong, holding his gaze as I continued. "You should have protected us. Instead, you forced us to ally with Azazel. We lost our free will because of you. We became monsters because of you. What you did is unforgivable, and you no longer deserve to be the leader of our pack. So now I—Sage Montgomery of the Montgomery pack—challenge you for the position of alpha."

33

SAGE

Flint did the last thing I expected him to do.

He laughed.

Maybe I *should* have expected that reaction. By having me abducted from my hunt with Noah, he'd certainly shown he didn't trust my decision-making skills in the slightest.

But it made no difference. Because I held my ground—and my gaze—against him.

He continued staring, daring me to look away and retract my challenge.

I didn't. I *wouldn't*.

The Montgomery pack deserved a better leader.

They deserved *me*.

"Who are you kidding here, Sage?" Flint finally

spoke. "I know you're angry at me, and rightly so. But you'd never kill your own brother."

"Challenges for the position of alpha don't have to be to the death," I said steadily. "You can bend the knee and declare me your alpha right now, and this won't have to get messy. Or we can fight until one of us yields. The choice is yours."

"Or you can drop this ridiculousness, go back to your princely vampire lover over there, and let me continue leading *my* pack." He snarled, glaring at Thomas. "You put her up to this, didn't you? You've always been power hungry. You've been a bad influence on her from the start."

"I haven't seen Sage—the *real*, not demon bound Sage —since you sent Azazel to abduct her while she was hunting our demon enemies in Chicago." Thomas remained calm as he replied to Flint. Then he smirked at me in approval. "This decision is all hers. And it's a fine one at that. I may not have put her up to it, but I certainly approve." He smiled at Flint, as if demonstrating that his gleaming teeth could be just as deadly as ours.

I didn't think it was possible, but with each word Thomas spoke, I loved him even more.

I wanted to kiss him right now. But I'd have plenty of

time to shower Thomas with my affections once this was sorted out.

So for now, I returned my focus to Flint. My brother looked more worried by the second.

"What'll it be?" I tilted my head, enjoying embarrassing him after everything he'd done to me and our pack. I'd enjoy it even more once I was alpha. "Bend the knee, or fight it out?"

He narrowed his red eyes at me, growled, and shifted into his wolf form.

Looked like we'd be fighting it out.

I shifted quickly, aware that Flint could use any extra seconds to launch an attack on me before I was ready. Which he *tried* to do, jumping forward and swatting at me with his claws. It wasn't a swat to kill, but it certainly would have hurt.

I dodged out of the way, and instead of getting me, he slashed at the air where I'd been standing.

Flint was bigger than me, both in human and wolf form, but *especially* in wolf form. And he was strong. But his size meant he had more weight to manage.

I was swift and nimble. I'd also been training with Noah while we'd been on the road together.

Growing up, Flint had always taught us how to defend—not to attack. We didn't need to know how to attack, because no one would dare threaten the Montgomery pack. We were basically royalty in the American shifter world, and the Hollywood Hills compound was our fortress. Why learn to attack when we already had all we could ever want?

I continued dodging all of Flint's attacks.

The first time my claw swiped his shoulder, he reared back in shock. Like it must have been a mistake.

When I managed to swipe his abdomen, he growled, fury raging further. I was fighting in a way he hadn't expected. And I was proud of myself for it.

Now I wondered if Flint had another reason for only teaching us defensive moves. Mainly, that he didn't want anyone challenging him for his position.

We circled each other, running toward each other to exchange blows. Everyone gasped and cheered as they watched in the circle surrounding us. I wasn't sure which one of us they were rooting for. And I didn't care.

Because I was in a groove now, expertly avoiding all of Flint's swipes and attempted bites. It was like a dance I was doing perfectly. The best part was that I was faster than him. My speed, combined with Noah's training, was giving me an advantage. Especially because Flint was getting angry.

My brother stopped thinking clearly when he got angry.

I didn't. I got more focused and more vicious. And after everything he'd done to me, I was more than angry.

I was *enraged*.

The third time I got in an attack—a bite to his leg—Flint swiped his paws angrily at my head. But he was too late. I'd been expecting the move. I'd already come around to his back and used all my body weight to push him into the ground.

He landed with an oomph as his breath left his chest.

I lowered my snout to his neck, opened my mouth, and bit down.

Not hard enough to kill. But hard enough to make my mark.

If this had been a fight to death, the bite easily could have been enough to kill. But despite all the awful things Flint had done to me recently, he was my brother. So, I let go once the telling teeth marks were there, and moved away to stand up.

A man of honor would realize this was the time to yield.

Flint wasn't a man of honor.

He launched at me to take me down.

But I'd been prepared for it. I knew my brother well. He wasn't going to yield easily.

He thought he had me, but I was ready. He flew past me, and a second later I had him on the ground again, my sharp, deadly claws pressed against his neck. I wrapped him in a tight hold that Noah had taught me.

No matter how much he tried to use his strength to push me off him, he wasn't going anywhere.

I dug my claws into his skin, drawing blood. Not so much blood that he'd die from it, but enough to show that I could kill him right now if that was my goal.

He still didn't yield.

So I dug in deeper. We couldn't speak as wolves, but as I stared down at him, I tried getting the message across with my eyes. I'd won this fight. I could hold him like this for hours. The more blood he lost, the weaker he'd become. Even with our accelerated healing, his blood would take time to replenish. He was too weak to stand a chance at a comeback.

He needed to yield. Now.

Because despite all the terrible things he'd done, I could never kill my own brother.

34

SAGE

I CONTINUED to hold Flint's gaze, willing him to stop being a stubborn idiot.

Finally, he shifted back to his human form. He stared at me in defeat, and I raised my claw from his neck.

"I yield," he croaked, reaching for the torn part of his neck as it started to heal.

I'd been hoping to hear those words. But it was a million times more thrilling when they were actually spoken out loud.

I shifted back into my human form and stood, holding out a hand to help Flint up.

He didn't take it. Instead he pushed himself up on his own, grunting from the pain of the injuries I'd inflicted on him as he did so. "Be alpha if you want," he said, his wounds dripping blood onto the grass as they closed. "It doesn't matter anyway, since the pack will be split between here and Avalon."

I simply stared him down, ignoring his jab as he walked over to Mara. His demon mate checked over his wounds, fawning over him to make sure he was okay.

He'd survive. His pride might never recover, but after what he'd put me and our pack through, he deserved it.

I stepped to the center of the circle, ready to take on my new position as alpha. "Does anyone here oppose me as your alpha?" I looked around at my pack mates, holding each of their gazes and only moving on after they looked away first. "If so, the time to challenge me is now."

No one spoke against me.

Which meant they accepted me as alpha.

Relief coursed through my body, although I didn't show it. It wouldn't do to let them see me as anything less than one hundred percent confident in this moment —and for all important moments moving forward.

Being alpha meant a lot of responsibility. But I was ready for it. Deep in my bones, I knew I'd been ready for years.

I just hadn't made any moves against Flint because I hadn't felt it right to take the position from him. Plus, before now, he hadn't done anything that had warranted me doing so. At least, not anything I was aware of.

But that was in the past. Now, it was time to focus on the future.

And with everyone gathered around me in a semicircle, it was time to share exactly what I had in mind for moving forward.

"Before hunting with Noah, I couldn't imagine leaving the home I'd known forever to go to Avalon," I started, knowing that what I was about to say needed to be said in a way that brought the pack together and didn't separate us. "But on the hunt, I discovered a sense of purpose. Because the demons that have broken into our world aren't going to live in the shadows forever. They have a plan. We saw a part of that plan when Azazel forced us to blood bind with him. We're beyond lucky—and grateful—that Raven killed him and returned our free will to us. And now that I know what it's like to have my free will taken away from me, I intend on doing everything I can to fight against the demons in the best way possible. Because we need to win this war. We *cannot* let the demons be victorious.

"The Earth Angel's army is based on Avalon." I glanced at Thomas briefly, and he nodded to assure me I had this. So I took a deep breath, and continued, "Therefore, it makes sense for everyone who wants to fight in that army—and against the demons—to go there. But if you don't want to fight, that's okay too. We're not all meant to be warriors. The different positions in a pack have always made that clear to us. And while I do intend to live on Avalon—if the island will have me—I won't abandon the Montgomery compound. I'll be stopping by regularly to check in on those of you who choose to stay behind. But now that we're at war with the demons for the first time in centuries, the world has become a darker, more dangerous place. So it's time for the compound to transform from our home into something greater." I paused and looked around again, wanting this next part to truly sink in and be as impactful as possible.

My pack—and the others from Avalon who had come to help us fight the demons—all looked at me with trusting gazes, waiting for what I had to say next.

"I want the compound to become a safe place for wild wolf shifters to come to learn how to acclimate to society," I said, glancing at Noah and shooting him a small smile. He looked surprised, but pleased with my decision. "Now that we're up against the demons, supernaturals need to band together—not remain apart. Yes, we'll be banding together on Avalon, but we need strongholds on Earth as well. Wild shifters like Noah might want to help us fight. They won't be able to do that if they're struggling to survive and sleeping on the streets, like Noah was when I first met him." I frowned at the memory of how lost Noah had been when I'd met him in the alley behind that supernatural dive bar in LA, and continued, "As you all know, it's not typical for civilized shifter packs to associate with wild shifter packs. The only reason Noah was allowed to stay at the compound earlier this year was because he saved my life, and our pack owed him a debt. Otherwise, he would have been sent back onto the streets." I paused, raising my voice to drive home my point. "That attitude ends today. Any wild wolf shifter who needs help—and who cooperates with us, of course—will be welcomed by the Montgomery wolves and will stay here for as long as they need. Understood?"

The crowd was a chorus of people saying yes. Noah's voice was the loudest.

My heart swelled, and I smiled, proud to be the alpha of my pack.

"What about me?" a small voice asked from off to the side. Kara. She looked so lost and confused that it made my heart hurt. "I don't want to stay here. But I was rejected from Avalon. Where do I belong now?"

I thought for a few seconds, knowing my pack was counting on me to say the right thing. "Where do you want to go?" I asked.

"Home." She glanced down at the ground and shuffled her feet in the dirt. "But now that I'm a vampire, I know that's not possible." She bit her lip, and continued, "Do you think the Haven would take me back?"

I thought back to Shivani's quick visit. Before flashing out, she'd reminded me that the Haven accepted any supernatural in need of a safe place.

Rosella must have told her that I'd need the reminder, so I'd be ready for this moment.

"I don't just *think* they'll take you back," I said, giving the young girl a warm smile. "I know they'll welcome you with open arms."

At that precise moment—likely because of Rosella's future sight—Shivani teleported back onto the yard. She searched the group for Kara and walked toward the young vampire.

"I hear you're interested in returning to the Haven?" she asked.

Kara simply nodded. She still looked lost, with a grief I knew would never truly pass because of the loss of her brother and because she'd never be able to return home.

But at least she had a new home now.

"Good. Because we'd love to have you back." Shivani lowered herself down so she was eye level with the girl and held out her hand. "Are you ready?"

Kara took the witch's hand, and Shivani teleported her back to the Haven.

I prayed Kara would eventually find happiness there. It would take time, but I believed she would.

Once they were gone, I refocused on the others standing in the yard. It was time to get back to business.

"With that taken care of, I need to know who's going to try going to Avalon, and who's going to remain here," I said. "I'll choose someone who's staying here to act as leader of the compound while I'm away. And then, those of us who want to join the Earth Angel's army will see if we're worthy of being accepted onto Avalon."

35

ANNIKA

I WAS happy to welcome the new arrivals from the Montgomery pack to Avalon—including Raven's mom Skylar and the vampire Derrick. It was especially exciting to meet Sage, after how much Thomas, Raven, and Noah had raved about her.

I trusted King Arthur's simulation. I really, truly did.

But I also couldn't help being skeptical that a *demon* had been accepted onto Avalon. It just wasn't normal that the very creature we were fighting was being allowed onto our sacred island. And the daughter of Azazel, no less. I'd heard all about how she'd gained a conscience after mating with the former alpha of the Montgomery pack. The entire island had heard the story by now, including the part where Mara had helped Skylar defeat her own father.

But I needed to see it to believe it.

Which was why after Darra's funeral pyre—a chilling ceremony where the witches sent her soul to the Beyond—I called for a meeting with Mara.

I wanted to make the demon girl comfortable, so I held the meeting in my quarters instead of the big round table in the throne room. But along with the guards stationed at the door, I had Jacen and Jessica there as well. Jacen for the emotional strength he gave me. Jessica because of her gift of sensing lies and getting people to tell the truth.

Mara curtseyed when she entered, and the four of us situated ourselves at the small table in my private dining room. Mara looked surprisingly unthreatening. She was petite, with long blonde hair and big eyes. If her eyes weren't demonic red, I might have said she looked innocent.

"Welcome to Avalon," I said, being diplomatic, as expected. "I hope you're finding it comfortable here."

"Very much so." She nodded and rested a hand on the teacup full of tea made with holy water. There was mana on the table as well, but none of us were eating. "Flint and I are grateful that Avalon accepted us, and I'm happy to be of assistance in any way you might need."

"That's good." I eyed her up, since this was the

moment of truth. "Because I have some questions for you."

"I figured as much." She straightened, ready for whatever was coming her way. It was impressive, considering how much pressure she must have been feeling right now.

I started with the basics, which consisted of confirming the story I'd been told so far. This also served to ease Mara into talking with me.

Jessica listened attentively, ready to jump in and ask a further question if Mara told a lie. That was going to be her signal to me that the demon wasn't being honest.

But Jessica was silent so far, which meant Mara was telling the truth.

Mara was now sipping her tea, apparently more comfortable now that we'd been chatting for a bit. Which meant it was time for the big question—the one we'd been wondering since the reconnaissance mission to the bunker.

"We discovered a container full of gifted vampire blood above the bunker where the gifted humans were being kept," I said. "We know the operation at the bunker was run by your father. What we want to know now is—why was he turning gifted humans into vampires and taking their blood?"

"I don't know." Mara shrugged and glanced down at

her tea. "I'm sorry."

I looked to Jessica.

She nodded. Mara was telling the truth.

"I don't understand," I prodded Mara further. "You mean to tell me that Azazel didn't tell you—his own daughter—what he was planning?"

"That's exactly what I mean," Mara said, her gaze sharper now. "My father didn't trust many people. After I imprinted on Flint, he kept a tighter tongue around me than usual. All I know is that whatever he was doing with the gifted humans, he was planning it with Lavinia Foster and my aunt Lilith."

"Lilith?" I repeated the name, dread swirling in my stomach. "I know that name from the Bible."

"That's the one," Mara confirmed. "The greater demon Lilith—sister to my father Azazel. She's out there, planning something. And before you ask me where she is, the answer is that I don't know. She kept her location hidden from everyone but my father and Lavinia. And if you thought my father was bad... well, he had nothing on my aunt."

Jessica remained silent.

Mara was telling the truth.

And it served as a reminder that while we'd won the battle with Azazel, the war against the demons was still far from over.

36

ANNIKA

SINCE MARA DIDN'T HAVE the information I needed, I sent her back to continue getting situated in her room with Flint. The Montgomery pack was living in one of the wooden cabins near the academy manor house. The cabins were large, but nowhere near as big as the mansions on the Montgomery compound. I hoped the Montgomery wolves were adjusting as well as Mara claimed they were.

I called for Violet, who was waiting with the guards outside my quarters. Out of all the mages, I related to her the most. She was the kindest of the three.

"Send a fire message to Skylar Danvers," I instructed. "I need to see her at once. Tell her to bring her tarot cards."

Violet did as asked, and Skylar arrived at my door

via a witch a few seconds later. I dismissed Jessica, since I trusted Skylar. Jacen remained, though. He co-led the island with me, and was with me for nearly all important matters.

The guards cleared Jessica and Mara's used dishes, cleaned up the table, and provided Skylar a fresh place setting. They also replaced the tea so it was hot again. Once all of that was done, they left the three of us alone.

"I heard the witches were able to brew a memory potion that made your friends and family forget that you and Raven have been gone for the past few months," I said, again starting with chitchat to make her feel comfortable.

"Yes," Skylar said. "They believe I got a job offer I couldn't refuse in New Zealand, and that Raven transferred to a university there."

"You'll visit them?" Jacen asked.

"Once or twice a year."

I nodded, pleased we'd found a solution that worked for them. And thanks to Thomas setting Avalon up with the Internet, our loved ones on Earth were always only a phone call or text message away.

Not that I had any loved ones left on Earth. My life was on Avalon now. But I was happy that everyone living on the island had a way of communicating with those they cared about.

Skylar placed her tarot deck on the table and removed the cards from the box. "I take it you asked me here to do a reading for you," she said.

"I did," I said, continuing on to fill her in on the gifted vampire blood and what Mara had told us about Lilith and Lavinia Foster working together. "I want to know what they're planning."

She shuffled the cards, fanned them out on the table, and picked one. The image was of a mystical looking, dark haired woman holding a large crystal ball. On the bottom of the card, it said, "The Unknown Card."

Skylar studied the card, looking perplexed.

"What's wrong?" I asked, although from the name of the card, I suspected she wouldn't be able to answer my question.

"The Unknown Card means the answer isn't meant to be revealed yet," she said, still focused on the card. "Usually, when I look at the cards, I see a vision in them that answers my question. Now, I'm only hearing something. Voices repeating the phrase, 'soon He will rise.'" She looked back up to me. "Do you have any idea what that means?"

"I've never heard it before," I said. "But how are we supposed to beat Lilith if we're not supposed to know what she's planning?"

"I'll ask the cards." Skylar hovered her hand over the

fanned out deck, going along the line until she stopped to pick a card. She placed it to the left of the Unknown Card. She picked three more cards the same way, placing another to the left of the Unknown Card, and the other two to the right.

I watched, fascinated, as she worked.

From left to right, the cards now were: the Queen of Cups, the Queen of Swords, the Unknown Card, the Queen of Wands, and the Queen of Pentacles. The women in each of the cards looked mature, strong, and confident. They all held a scepter or a sword.

I didn't know anything about tarot, but the fact that she'd pulled all queens had to be significant.

Skylar studied the cards intensely now. It was like she was watching a video on a tablet, but I couldn't hear or see what she was viewing.

Jacen and I remained silent, waiting for her to be ready to share. I barely moved, afraid that any sound might distract her from what she was seeing.

Finally, she looked up from the cards, her gaze intense when it met mine. "As you know, the future is never set in stone," she began. "I see the most likely future at any point in time, but that can always change. Azazel proved as much when he used my visions to alter the future to his liking."

"I know," I said, since Rosella had told me as much back when I'd first met her in the Haven.

"The queens in the cards represent the four women who must rise to power and join forces to defeat the demons," she said. "The queens to the left of the Unknown Card—the Queen of Cups and Queen of Swords—have already risen." Her gaze sharpened as she looked at me. "When I looked into the card, I saw the moment you drank from the Holy Grail in Heaven. You are the Queen of Cups."

I gulped as I looked at the card. It showed a woman with long blonde hair holding a trident scepter, with the Holy Grail sitting by her side. "She doesn't look like me," I said.

"Every tarot deck uses different art to portray the cards," Skylar explained. "The artwork of my deck may not look like you. But when I looked into the card, I saw you drinking from the Grail. You are the Queen of Cups. There's no doubt about it."

I glanced over at Jacen. He sat back casually in his chair, looking annoyingly entertained.

"What's so funny?" I asked him.

"When we arrived on Avalon, you said you were done with royals and were banishing all royal titles from the island," he said. "But apparently that wasn't meant to be. Was it?"

"It wasn't meant to be," Skylar agreed. "Annika is a queen, whether she asks others to address her by her title or not."

I pursed my lips together, saying nothing. Jacen was never going to let me hear the end of this.

"You will continue to use the Holy Grail to create Nephilim, and they will fight in the war against the demons," Skylar said. "Your accomplishments so far were integral for our success in this war. None of us would be here today if not for you."

"And the other queens?" I focused on the Queen of Swords, since her card was also to the left of the Unknown Card. "Who's the other one that's already risen?"

"That would be Raven," Skylar said, which didn't surprise me, given that Excalibur had risen from the lake for her. "Her gift of stubbornness allowed her to survive drinking pure angel blood from the Grail to become the first of a new generation of Nephilim. Her blood will be used in the Grail moving forward, since it's not so potent that it will kill, but it's still strong enough to do the job. But I urge you to keep her as humble as you are about your title as queen. We don't want it getting to her head."

"We certainly don't," I agreed, although Raven was so strong-minded that she'd react to the news of being a queen however she saw fit. "What about the queens who still haven't risen?" I asked, turning my focus to the cards on the right. The Queen of Wands and Queen of Pentacles. The Queen of Wands held a beautiful scepter wand topped with a glowing red stone, and the Queen of Pentacles sat in front of a tree surrounded by white crystal wands, a pentacle scepter in her hand. "How will we find them?"

"That's another question for the cards," Skylar said, letting her hand linger above the ones fanned out on the table again. She picked another card and laid it above the others.

On the card was a young woman dressed in a flowing pink dress. She stood at the edge of a cliff, about to step over it. Butterflies surrounded her. The bottom of the card said The Fool.

Skylar watched this card as closely as she'd watched the ones with the queens.

After about thirty seconds, she looked back up to me. "The other two queens haven't started their journeys yet," she said. "They haven't even been born yet."

"What?" I gasped, since that wasn't what I'd expected to hear. "How long will we have to wait for them to be born?"

Really, what I was wondering was—how long would this war with the demons last? Because with the other queens not born yet, we could be in for an extraordi-narily long wait. Decades, or perhaps even longer.

That would be a hard blow to everyone living and training on Avalon.

"Not long," she said with a knowing smile. Her words eased my concerns slightly. "The queens will have many adventures and choices to come. They're up for the task—they wouldn't have been chosen as queens otherwise. But it's up to those of us on Avalon to be ready for them once they arrive. We need to continue training your army and killing demons on Earth who threaten humans as we wait for the other two queens to join us."

We all three sat there in silence, taking it the enor-mity of what we'd just learned.

"Thank you, Skylar," I said. "I'm glad you're here on Avalon. Your gift is going to be extremely helpful in the times ahead. I appreciate you willingly sharing it with us."

"I'm happy to help in whatever ways I can." She gath-ered up the cards, collecting them into a neat pile in her hand. "Is there anything else you need from me right now?"

"That will be all," I said.

"I hope we didn't take you away from wedding plan-ning for too long," Jacen added.

"No." Skylar smiled, standing up after Jacen and I did. "But Raven's never been the best with figuring out details. So I'll be getting back to helping her right away."

"As you should." I glanced down at my own engagement ring, since theirs wasn't the only wedding approaching. "The wedding is just what Avalon needs right now. We can't wait to celebrate with you."

"And I with you," Skylar said, the two of us sharing a mutual look of excitement and anticipation.

With that, I saw Skylar out, glad to be alone with Jacen so we could discuss everything we'd just learned about the four queens and the war to come.

37

RAVEN

I COULDN'T WAIT to marry and mate with Noah, and Sage couldn't wait to marry and mate with Thomas.

Given everything the four of us had been through together, a double wedding felt like the most natural decision of all. We were combining a traditional human wedding with a traditional shifter mating ceremony. It gave us the best of both worlds, and symbolized our lives and cultures becoming one.

And now, the big day was finally here.

We got ready for the ceremony in a warm, welcoming room in the main castle. The mages had spelled a special wardrobe just for the occasion. It produced dream wedding dresses for both of us.

I'd never stop being amazed by how incredible their magic was.

Sage's dress was tight and daring. It cut deep into her chest and had a slit going all the way up her thigh. On her head was a flower crown of sage flowers mixed with baby's breath, bringing out her earthy, shifter side. The tall, white stilettos on her feet looked like potential death traps, but of course she walked in them with perfect grace.

My dress was the complete opposite. It had enough poof that Cinderella would be proud, although the top part was tight and fitting, with an explosion of silver crystals befitting the Queen of Swords. I'd taken the new title to heart. I even wore a gorgeous diamond and pearl queen's crown on my head, paired with matching earrings that fell nearly to my neck.

Perfect for a queen.

But the best part of the ensemble was that because my feet were hidden, I was wearing Converse sneakers and no one would ever know the difference. Beauty and comfort made a winning combination.

Adriana—the vampire from the Tower who'd been icy to Jessica on our first day at Avalon Academy—did hair and makeup for both of us. I wore my hair in a royal up-do at the nape of my neck, since the crown needed to fit on the top of my head. Sage had hers flowing in loose waves.

Adriana had warmed up to us as much as she could,

given that she wasn't the warmest person to begin with. And while I doubted I'd be considering her a close friend anytime soon, there was no denying that she knew what she was doing with hair and makeup. She'd been the fashion coordinator for the royals at the Tower Kingdom for a reason, and that reason showed once she was done with us.

My mom sat in the room as well, chatting and helping us calm our nerves as we got ready. Sage's parents had both been killed when she was ten in a fight with a rogue vampire coven, and my mom was happy to accept Sage as an honorary daughter after learning the truth about how much Sage had looked out for me after my mom had been taken by Azazel.

Once it was time, Iris fetched us and walked us out to the courtyard. Iris was planning and running the entire wedding, and she'd done an incredible job. There was a reason why this was her job on Avalon, and her amazing planning skills had made the days leading up to the wedding a breeze.

Sage and I arrived once the ceremony had already begun, since we didn't want our fiancés—soon to be husbands—to see us in our dresses until we walked down the aisle. No one could see us yet, thanks to an invisibility spell placed on us by Iris. But we could see everything, and the courtyard was breathtaking.

Strings of fairy lights were strung from one side of the castle to the other, giving a canopy effect across the entire courtyard. The white covered seats were all lit up, with huge bouquets of azaleas on the aisle at each row. Somehow, the central courtyard was big enough to hold every citizen of Avalon. I suspected mage magic made that happen. The aisle was covered in a sea of white rose petals.

The arch at the front, where Annika was officiating the service, was draped with sheer white tulle lit up from behind. It looked like a magical gazebo.

And standing under the arch was the man who took my breath away every time I saw him—Noah. I knew suits weren't his thing—he preferred jeans and a t-shirt —but he looked incredibly handsome in the one he was wearing right now.

Iris led my mom, Sage, and me to the start of the aisle. Since we were still invisible, no one had turned to look at us yet. They had no idea we were there.

The aisle was more than wide enough for three people, and my mom laced her arms around Sage's and mine. She held onto both of us at the elbow.

My heart filled with happiness. Having my mom here with me today, and knowing how supportive she was of Noah and me, meant more than I could ever say.

"Are you all ready?" Iris asked with a raised eyebrow.

She brought her hands together, excited for what was coming next.

"Yes," Sage said, her eyes locked on Thomas. They shined with love—the same way I was sure mine did as I looked at Noah.

"I'm ready." My heart beat with excitement and anticipation. Butterflies fluttered in my stomach. They were good butterflies—the type of nervous you get when you know you're about to experience one the most meaningful moments of your life.

The music started. Then Iris raised her hands, and a bright ring of yellow sparklers—large enough for three people to step through—lit up in a circle front of us.

We stepped through, and the ring of sparklers stripped away the invisibility spell, making us visible to the crowd.

Everyone stood and sucked in deep breaths of awe.

But I wasn't looking at them.

Because as I walked down the aisle, my eyes were fixed on Noah's, as his were on me.

This was it. This was forever.

And I'd never been happier.

38

RAVEN

THE CEREMONY WAS PERFECT.

Afterward, we gathered in the ballroom for the beautiful reception my mom and Iris had planned. The inside was just as fairytale perfect as they'd said it would be. A wedding fit for royalty.

Which made sense, since Sage and Noah were alphas, Thomas was a vampire prince, and I was the Queen of Swords. We were quite the fearsome foursome.

I tried my best to enjoy the reception. It wasn't easy, because every bone in my body ached to go to the room in the castle that had been prepared for Noah and me so we could complete the mating ceremony.

But of course we stayed until send off, enjoying every last moment of this perfect evening.

Per shifter tradition, Noah's beta—Gabriel—and the eldest woman in the pack—Sarah—walked us to our mating room. Noah and I held hands the entire way through the halls and up the steps.

We all stopped at the carved wooden double doors leading into the room that had been prepared for the night. I was going to move into the Southern Vale pack's cabin after the wedding, but for tonight, the Earth Angel wanted us to have this special room. A "honeymoon suite," since a honeymoon wasn't on our agenda at the moment, given all we had to do on Avalon.

Gabriel and Sarah pushed open the doors to the room. It was gorgeous. With a red canopy bed in the center, a Turkish rug laid out across the entire floor, and a fireplace already glowing, the suite was warm, luxurious, and welcoming. I couldn't think of a more perfect place to share this night with Noah.

We stepped inside, basking in the majestic aura of it all.

"Like it?" Noah asked, looking to me for approval.

"I love it." I smiled at him, unable to believe this was my real life. "It's perfect. And I love you."

I felt Noah's emotions through the imprint bond, but his dark, intense gaze said it all. He loved me, and he wanted to make our mating bond official. Now.

Mischief shined in Sarah's eyes as she looked back and forth between us. "We'll be leaving the two of you alone now," she said, and she and Gabriel backed away, closing the doors behind them.

Now it was just us.

Both of our hearts pounded quickly. I knew because with my new superhuman senses, I could hear them.

Noah gazed into my eyes, looking at me with love, awe, and respect. "Finally," he said.

"Finally," I repeated.

Electricity buzzed between us. We couldn't hold back anymore. And the best part was, we didn't have to.

So he took me in his arms, carried me over to the bed, and finally, we sealed the bond between us.

We held each other in the luxurious bed, the fire in the mantel long since gone out. I was tracing my fingers along Noah's perfect face when I noticed something huge.

His eyes weren't the same brown they'd always been.

"Your eyes," I said, unable to believe it.

"What about my eyes?" he asked, amused. "You love them too?"

He was referencing a time slightly earlier that night, when I'd told him how much I loved every single part of him—and shown him, too. He'd then done the same, before we'd again shown how much we loved each other, as we had many times during the night.

"Of course I do." I smiled. "Always. But they've changed. They have a ring of gold around them. Like mine."

Surprise, followed by happiness, spread across his face. He stood and walked across the room to the mirror on the wall, examining his reflection. "So," he said, turning and rushing back to join me in the bed. "Looks like I'm Nephilim now."

"Looks like it," I said.

We were both being so casual about it, but I could feel the mutual excitement bursting through both of our veins.

After witnessing what had happened to Mara and Flint, we'd suspected this might be a possibility. But we couldn't know for sure, since shifters originated from demons, whereas shifters and Nephilim were completely different entities.

"Can you feel a wolf inside you?" he asked.

"I feel wildness inside me." I smirked, tossing my hair behind my back. "Is that the same?"

Before he could answer, I covered his mouth with

mine, and went in for round… well, I'd lost track by that point.

Once we were both holding each other again, he cocked his head to the side, amused. "That wildness you mentioned could be your wolf," he said. "Hold out your hand." He traced his fingers from the top of my arm, to my elbows, until finally reaching my hand. "See if you can shift your fingers into claws."

I held my hand out and stared at it. "What do I do?" I asked. "Just… imagine my fingers turning into claws?"

"Call on your wolf within you," he said. "And yes, picture your fingers turning into claws."

I did as he said, searching inward to find my wolf. The flames burning from my stomach were hotter than ever, as if the animal side of me was bursting to break free.

I studied my hand intensely and pictured it turning into claws, like I'd seen Noah and Sage's hands do when they'd shifted in front of me.

Within a second, my fingers extended outward into claws.

Within a few more seconds, my entire point of view shifted. I was standing on all fours as I gazed down at Noah, my senses heightened even more than they were since turning Nephilim. I could see everything, hear everything… I could even *taste* the distinct, woodsy taste of Noah in the air. It was incredible.

"Raven," Noah said, his golden eyes wide in amazement. "You're beautiful."

I hopped over to the full-length mirror, beyond curious about what I'd see.

As expected, the face staring back at me wasn't mine. It was a wolf. A majestic wolf with Nephilim yellow eyes and red fur that matched my hair.

I was a dyad. Noah, too. Nephilim-wolf shifter dyads. No one like us had ever existed in the history of the world.

The Earth Angel was going to be thrilled about what our new species would bring to the war with the demons.

But tonight wasn't about war. Tonight was about love. Specifically, the love between Noah and me.

I thought of myself as human, and in a few seconds, I was back to human form.

"That's amazing," Noah said. "It usually takes newbies a few times to master the shift."

"Maybe I'm a natural because I'm Nephilim." I sauntered over to him on the bed, swaying my hips more than normal to tease him.

"You're certainly a natural at many things," he said

with a devilish grin, his eyes wandering along every inch of my body.

"I love you," I said.

"And I love you." He pulled me back to the bed with him, our faces close as we gazed into each other's eyes with the kind of pure love that I was convinced could only exist between mates. "Forever."

39

ANNIKA

TWO MONTHS LATER

EVER SINCE RAVEN BECAME NEPHILIM, five humans had passed the Angel Trials and drank her blood from the Holy Grail. They all survived the transition.

It turned out the Trials accurately predicted who was strong enough to drink from the Grail and survive, after all. We just needed them to drink Nephilim blood instead of my pure angel blood.

It was a good thing that Raven was strong and stubborn enough to survive drinking my blood from the Grail. Without her, an army of Nephilim wouldn't have been possible.

Sure, we didn't have an army of Nephilim yet.

But we'd get there.

And once we did, the demons would get what was coming to them.

In the meantime, I had something more important to focus on. Because after a lot of soul healing, and a long engagement to Jacen—who was incredibly understanding as he waited for me to accept that the deaths of the humans before Raven weren't my fault—the big day was finally here.

Our wedding.

The ceremony and reception were held at a lake in a valley surrounded by majestic green mountains. We wanted our wedding to show our connection to the island, while being different from Raven and Noah's and Sage and Thomas's double wedding in the castle.

Iris did an incredible job planning it. There was no better way to show our connection to the island than to marry each other surrounded by its breathtaking nature. The ceremony was timed with sunset, cocktail hour happened at twilight, and night descended when the reception began. My dress was even adorned with large white feathers, making me look every bit an angel.

Jacen and I had just finished our first dance, and others were getting up to join us on the dance floor, when someone screamed from one of the tables.

Camelia.

She stood with one hand on the table, and the other on her pregnant stomach. There was a puddle of water around her feet.

Her water had broken. The baby was coming.

Camelia wasn't due for another month. But it looked like that baby girl of hers couldn't handle the thought of all of us partying without her.

Violet and Dahlia teleported to Camelia's side in an instant.

"We'll take Camelia to her chambers and help welcome her baby girl into the world." Dahlia smiled, sounding as chipper as ever. "What an incredible night! Two joyous milestones at once."

With that, she and Violet disappeared with Camelia. All that was left where they'd been standing was the puddle of water that had been at Camelia's feet.

I stood in there in a strange state of shock. Because that was the last thing I'd expected to happen at my wedding. A demon attack, sure. But the first birth on Avalon? I hadn't been ready for that.

Hopefully everything would go well with the delivery of the baby. I trusted that Camelia was in excellent hands with the mages. But still, I worried.

Iris was up on the stage at once. "Why so quiet?" she asked with a chuckle, putting everyone at ease. "We have the rest of the night to continue celebrating the union of our founders, the Earth Angel Annika and Prince Jacen. Tomorrow, we'll celebrate Camelia's baby girl. So…" She turned to look at Eric, a human from the

Academy who was manning the DJ table. "Let the party continue!"

I tried to enjoy the rest of my wedding reception. I really, truly did.

But I couldn't get rid of the feeling that something wasn't right. Jacen tried distracting me, although the feeling remained. I think I did a good job at hiding it from everyone else. But the truth was, I was still worried for Camelia.

I shouldn't have been worried for her, since she'd been an evil witch to me during my time in the Vale. But something bad was happening. I knew it deep in my soul.

And as an angel, my intuition was rarely wrong.

After the last dance—and yes, we opted to have the song "Last Dance" play for our last dance—a fire message appeared in Iris's hands. She opened the paper and read the message, her forehead wrinkling in concern.

She closed it and walked over to where Jacen and I stood in the center of the dance floor. "My sisters need you and Prince Jacen in Camelia's chambers at once," she said, low enough to make it clear that she was saying this only for us. At a party with mostly supernaturals, others were bound to overhear, but etiquette demanded they pretended they didn't. "It's an emergency."

"I understand," I said, since Dahlia and Violet wouldn't have called us away from our own wedding for anything else. "Take care of seeing everyone out. I'll see you soon."

Iris bowed her head in acknowledgement of my order.

Then I reached for Jacen's hand, and teleported the two of us to Camelia's chambers.

40

ANNIKA

CAMELIA HELD a beautiful baby girl in her arms. The child's hair was so blonde it was nearly white.

She gazed down at her baby adoringly, and the baby looked up at her in wonder, like she was amazed at the existence of the world.

It would have been a perfect scene, if not for the massive amounts of blood that drenched Camelia's sheets. There was so much blood that the sheets looked red instead of white. And Camelia's complexion was pale—too pale.

Violet hurried over to me, and Dahlia remained by Camelia's side.

If Camelia noticed that Jacen and I had just arrived in her chambers, she didn't show it. She was too focused on the beautiful newborn baby girl in her arms.

And the baby girl herself… she had a scent I wasn't familiar with. The flowery smell of witch was obvious. But there was something else. A rich, creamy smell. Like vanilla.

I'd never encountered such a smell from any supernatural I'd met yet.

That had to be what the fae smelled like. I'd never met a fae—neither had most other supernaturals, since the fae kept to themselves in the Otherworld. But I knew the father of Camelia's child was a fae. That was why I'd permitted Camelia to live on Avalon in the first place.

Back when we were all living at the Vale, Camelia had made a deal with the fae. The deal had resulted in her getting pregnant with a half-fae child and promising that child—this beautiful baby girl she was cradling—to the fae.

As a half-blood fae in the Otherworld, this child would always be treated like a second-class citizen there. She would be denied full rights simply because of the circumstance of her birth. Avalon was the only place where Camelia and the child would be safe, as the blessing on the island prevented anyone—even the fae— from locating it. And even if they did locate it, as Kara had done, King Arthur's simulation kept them from entering.

Therefore, I'd overcome my grudges against Camelia and had allowed her to come to the island. Her child deserved a life in a place where she'd have every opportunity to grow and shine to her full potential. She also deserved her mother, no matter how evil and conniving her mother had acted in the past.

But looking at Camelia now, I wasn't sure how much time she had left.

"She's lost so much blood," I said to Violet, dread mounting in my stomach at the sight of the blood stained sheets. I didn't want to stare at the blood, but I couldn't turn away.

"Dahlia and I did everything we could," Violet said softly, turning her gaze down to the floor. "But the blood loss is too extreme for healing potion to fix."

I nodded and swallowed down a lump in my throat. Because I, like all other supernaturals, knew how healing potion worked. It only healed non-fatal injuries. And while vampire blood could be used to heal fatal injuries in humans—a fact that vampires kept hidden, since they didn't want to be hunted for their blood—it had no effect on other supernaturals.

If healing potion wasn't working on Camelia, her death was imminent. And judging by how she was now slumped in her pillow, using what appeared to be her last strength to hold her baby, she didn't have much longer.

After everything Camelia had done to me in the Vale —including having my two closest friends killed—I should have wanted her dead. But seeing the joy on her face as she looked down at her newborn baby girl, my heart was heavy with sadness.

Camelia finally raised her gaze from the child, her glazed eyes meeting mine. "Her name is Selena," she said, each word sounding like it took great effort to speak. "And I want to give her to you."

41

ANNIKA

"ARE YOU SURE?" I couldn't believe this. Camelia hated me. Why would she choose Jacen and me, of all people, to raise her child?

Anger flared in Camelia's eyes. It was the first surge of strength I'd seen from her since entering the room. "You don't want her?" she asked.

I hurried over to Camelia's bed, Jacen by my side. One look at him confirmed he was thinking the same thing as me.

We loved the beautiful baby girl in Camelia's arms as fiercely as if we'd conceived her ourselves.

We'd never be able to conceive our own child, since Jacen was a vampire. We had been considering adopting at some point, but we hadn't thought of timing beyond that.

It looked like that point was now.

"We want her," I said, speaking for both of us. "I'm just surprised you'd entrust us with someone so important to you. I thought you hated us."

"Oh, I do hate you." Camelia chuckled, although she groaned from pain afterward. She looked from me to Jacen and back again. "I hate both of you. But you're the best people to raise her. You're the leaders of the most powerful supernatural island in the world, which means you're equipped to keep her safe and protected. And most importantly, you'll love her and give her the life she deserves."

"We will." Jacen placed a hand gently on Camelia's arm, his eyes shining with love for the baby girl she was holding. *Our* baby girl. "We promise."

"Yes." I nodded, more love swelling in my heart for Selena than I'd ever imagined possible. "We promise."

Selena was so beautiful—I ached to reach out and touch her. But I held back. Because Jacen and I had the rest of our lives with her. Camelia only had these final moments.

"But there's one condition," Camelia added.

The edge in her tone made my guard go up.

It was amazing how Camelia could still sound fierce, even while she was dying.

"What's that?" I asked.

"Everyone in this room must enter into a blood oath to never tell Selena that I bargained her away to the fae," Camelia said, her eyes dark as she held her baby girl closer to her chest. "No assisting her in finding out the truth on her own, either. You *must* keep Selena on Avalon—otherwise the fae will snatch her away. But she can't know why. Don't even tell her the truth about what she is."

"I can't promise that," I said, since how could I tell such a huge lie to my own daughter? She'd be unable to leave Avalon, yet she'd never know why. It wouldn't be fair. Plus, she'd have faerie powers. She'd eventually want to know who her biological father was, and why he wasn't in her life. She might even want to seek him out herself. In which case, she'd need to go in fully prepared with the knowledge of the bargain Camelia made on her behalf.

"I agree with Annika," Jacen said. "We'll love Selena, always. And we'll be the best parents to her that we can. But that means being honest with her about who she is and why she can't leave Avalon."

"Then I'm afraid we don't have a deal." Camelia held the crown of Selena's head tightly with one hand. "If you don't make this promise, I'll take Selena to the Beyond with me."

My eyes widened. She couldn't mean…

"No." I sat forward, but Camelia's sharp gaze warned me not to get closer. So I didn't. But only for Selena's sake. "You wouldn't."

"I wouldn't snap her neck so she can be in the Beyond with me, instead of growing up knowing that her mother bargained her away to a place where she'd be treated like dirt?" Camelia's eyes narrowed in challenge. "Watch me."

My heart pounded, terrified as I looked at my innocent baby girl. One quick move of Camelia's, and I could lose my daughter before ever holding her.

"Stop." I held my hands out in defeat, unable to take this. "We'll do it. We'll make the blood oath. Just… don't hurt Selena. Please."

"I thought so." Camelia smiled, although she kept her hand where it was on Selena's head. "Everyone, gather around."

"Hand Selena over first," Jacen said. "Then we'll make the blood oath."

"You think I'd fall for that?" Camelia looked at him like he was dirt.

"No," Jacen said. "But it was worth a try."

Camelia watched as Dahlia, Violet, Jacen, and I gathered around her bed. None of us made any sudden movements. Even though we were all quick and Camelia was dying, we couldn't risk Selena's life.

"Good," Camelia said, pleased that we were doing as she asked. "Let's begin."

She had Violet slice her palm, keeping her other hand tightly wound around Selena's head the entire time. Once her palm was sliced, we each sliced our own palms. Then, Camelia repeated the terms from before.

We couldn't tell Selena she was half fae. We couldn't tell Selena that Camelia had bargained her away to the fae. We couldn't tell Selena who her father was. We couldn't help Selena discover the truth on her own. The requirements continued, the oath airtight.

Reluctantly, we all pressed our bloodied palms to Camelia's, sealing the deal. I felt the buzz of the magic searing through my veins, binding me to keep my word.

The promise sealed, and with it, the cuts on our palms sealed as well.

"It's done," Camelia said, her hand still wrapped around the crown of Selena's head. "Selena is yours. But first... my Final Spell."

"What do you mean?" We'd already done what Camelia had wanted. Now every bone in my body screamed for her to hand Selena over to Jacen and me, so Selena would be safe.

Camelia closed her eyes and started muttering in Latin. As she did, yellow magic ebbed out from her, encompassing her and Selena into a glowing bubble. She kept muttering the words I didn't understand, the magic getting brighter and brighter.

She stopped speaking, and the magic hurtled away from her, going straight into Selena. It hummed around the tiny baby until every last bit of it dissolved into her.

Once all the magic was gone, Camelia lowered Selena gently to her lap, leaned back on the bed, and closed her eyes. Her breathing stopped.

Camelia was gone.

And Selena no longer smelled like warm vanilla. All that was left was the familiar floral scent of witch.

The scent of the fae had disappeared.

I lifted Selena gently off Camelia's body, cradling her in my arms and examining her to make sure she was okay.

She was more than okay—she was beautiful. Her eyes were a stunning deep violet that I'd never seen before. And she looked up at me with so much love that it filled my heart more than I ever thought possible.

Today I hadn't only become a wife—I'd become a mother as well. I was so happy I feared I might burst.

Jacen moved next to me, placing a hand protectively over Selena's head. "What did Camelia do to her?" he asked, looking to Dahlia and Violet for the answer.

"Camelia used her Final Spell to bind Selena's faerie side," Dahlia said, stunned as she looked at the baby girl in my arms. "Selena's faerie magic is still inside of her—no witch spell could ever take that away—but it's dormant. She won't be able to access it."

"For how long?" I asked.

"For forever," Violet said. "Perhaps one of the fae would be able to reverse the spell, but given the circumstances of Selena's situation..." She let the sentence hang, looking at Selena with sadness.

"The fae can never know Selena exists." I held her closer, protecting her. Selena was my daughter. I was going to keep her safe no matter what.

Even if that meant she never knew about half of who she was.

"The fae will never find her." Jacen gazed into my eyes, love for Selena and me radiating off every bit of him. "We'll keep her safe on Avalon. They won't take her away from us. She's ours, and she'll always be safe here."

"I love you," I said, nestling into him so we could both admire our beautiful daughter.

"And I love you," he said. "Both of you. For all of our lives, and into the Beyond."

"Yes," I said, positive it was impossible to feel any more joy than I was feeling right now. "The two of you are my family, and Avalon is our home. We'll live here, together. Forever."

Thank you for reading The Angel Test! The Angel Trials series has been a blast to write, and I hope you've loved it much as I loved writing it.

But the series isn't over yet! As a gift for my readers, I've written an epilogue. It's an *epic* epilogue from the point of view of Selena's father, Prince Devyn, at the moment Selena was born. It'll give you more insight about what's coming in the next season—Dark World: The Faerie Games. And it's a big reveal. So you definitely don't want to miss it.

To grab the epic epilogue, CLICK HERE or visit www.michellemadow.com/angeltestepilogue!

You'll be subscribing to my email list to get the epilogue. I love connecting with my readers and promise not to spam you, but you're free to unsubscribe at any time.

While The Angel Trials is over, there are still more seasons left in the Dark World universe. Get ready for Selena's story in season three, The Faerie Games, coming late summer 2019. And brace yourself, because it's going to be a wild, magical ride!

To receive an email alert from me when The Faerie Games is live on Amazon, CLICK HERE or visit www. michellemadow.com/subscribe and sign up for my newsletter.

To receive a Facebook message from me when The Faerie Games is live on Amazon, CLICK HERE or visit manychat.com/L2/michellemadow.

If you haven't read the first season of the Dark World Saga yet—The Vampire Wish—I recommend checking it out while you wait for The Faerie Games. It's about Annika and how she became the Earth Angel/Queen of Cups. And it's available in a box set, so it's a fantastic deal! (You might have to turn the page to view the cover and description.)

This box set includes all five books in The Vampire Wish series by USA Today bestselling author Michelle Madow and is over 1,200 pages of magic, romance, adventure, and twists you'll never see coming.

Annika never thought of herself as weak—until vampires murdered her parents and kidnapped her to their hidden kingdom of the Vale.

As a brand new blood slave, Annika must survive her dangerous new circumstances—or face death from the wolves prowling the Vale's enchanted walls. But sparks fly when she meets the vampire prince Jacen. She hates the idea of falling for the enemy, but her connection with the mysterious prince could be the key to her freedom.

Because if she can convince him to turn her into a vampire, she'll finally have the strength she needs to escape the Vale.

Thousands of copies sold. Millions of pages read. 700+ five-star reviews for the series. Now, for a limited time, save 50% compared to buying the individual books by reading the entire Vampire Wish series in this special bundle deal!

Price for all five books separately: $18.95
Price for all five books in the box set: $9.99*
That's less than $2 per book!

Check out The Vampire Wish: The Complete Series in your preferred format on Amazon:

Kindle ➜ CLICK HERE
Paperback ➜ CLICK HERE
Audio ➜ CLICK HERE

*Special pricing offer is only for the Kindle version. Pricing will vary for the paperback and audio formats.

ABOUT THE AUTHOR

Michelle Madow is a USA Today bestselling author of fast paced fantasy novels that will leave you turning the pages wanting more! Her books are full of magic, adventure, romance, and twists you'll never see coming.

Click here or visit author.to/MichelleMadow to view a full list of Michelle's novels on Amazon.

To get free books, exclusive content, and instant updates from Michelle, visit www.michellemadow.com/subscribe and subscribe to her newsletter now!

THE ANGEL SECRET

Published by Dreamscape Publishing

Copyright © 2019 Michelle Madow

ISBN: 9781098723040

❀ Created with Vellum